TIME WATCH

KATE ALLENTON

Published by Coastal Escape Publishing

Discover other titles by Kate Allenton
At

http://www.kateallenton.com

❀ Created with Vellum

1

"By any means necessary." Sarah Weston repeated the orders in her mind, driving home the point as if it would make her future actions seem less barbaric. She swallowed around the lump in her throat. This was the part of the job she hated. She understood the reasoning; but she hated it nonetheless.

The air in the alley charged and sizzled to life. Blue and white electrical currents danced between the concrete buildings, grounding and creating until it formed a circular live current floating in midair, big enough for an adult-sized person to step through. Sarah crossed the time slip's threshold.

She wasn't maneuvering through time, although that was also a capable function of biofeed meter attached to her wrist. She had no desire to visit other time frames. She'd mastered the scientific secret of the time slip as a quick way to travel from point A to point B in her first year on the job. Arriving fast to a crisis like this wasn't just for convenience but out of necessity.

She molded the loose platinum strands of hair that had escaped her bun before tugging at the hem of her white jacket, straightening her business suit. Her gaze darted around the location and nose twitched at the overbearing stench of urine and rotted food wafting from the stuffed dumpsters. Trash and debris littered the sticky ground as a rat squealed while scurrying by Sarah's designer heels. She emerged from the alley's shadow and glanced up and down the unfamiliar street, getting her bearings.

Women dressed like hookers were on one street corner and kids with jeans hanging so low she could see their boxers were standing in front of a convenience store.

The weathered and aged motel sign hung askew, several fluorescent bulbs blown out. Sarah didn't need to read the hotel name to figure she was in the right location. She'd followed the trail.

Sarah yanked the door open and stepped inside the dingy lobby. Stale, pungent air smacked her in the face. She would need to shower for days to wash away the remnants of this assignment.

Jonathan had arrived before her and stood with his back to the lobby door. He turned as if smelling the stench of her arrival and the stink clinging to her pores. The stone veneer on his familiar face softened into a warm smile. His dark hair hung down his brow. His blue eyes sparkled with mischief. Jonathan had a love for the chase.

Jonathan and Sarah worked well together, better than most in an industry so far off the grid that normal humans couldn't comprehend it. STEM Corp's scientists were responsible for several things, time travel was just one of the more exciting pursuits they monitored. The lab was situated on the outskirts of New York on ten acres away from prying eyes. No one would even believe they had their thumb on the pulse of something still believed to only exist in Science Fiction books.

Sarah and Jonathan's responsibilities at STEM Corp included; babysitter, concierge, and occasional bouncer, just to name a few. They weren't the inventors of time travel, or any other miraculous discoveries, but their job was just as important.

She and five other analysts made sure everything ran smoothly and under the radar with the twenty time travelers doing research in the current year. The reason Sarah and Jonathan were taking this trip into Little China Town was to stop one of the time travelers from exposing their anonymity.

A man dressed in jeans and an untucked shirt walked toward her. His greasy hair was cleaner than the look he was giving her. His eyes lingered on

Sarah's silk blouse as if undressing her in his mind. Words in a foreign tongue washed over her.

Sarah punched a button on her biofeed watch, engaging the language translator implant and effectively translating his speech from Chinese into English.

The small cylinder implant worked like a computer chip, engaging parts of the brain to translate words into something recognizable. The agency implanted all time travelers upon arriving and workers when hired to bridge the language gap.

His words were now understood easily. "I'd like to get you on your knees."

"You'd lose your family jewels." She bared her teeth and then chomped, giving him the universal sign he could understand.

Jonathan held the elevator door for Sarah to enter. "Are you sure Crenshaw is here? I did an initial biofeed sweep, and I'm not picking up any signals."

Biofeeds served many purposes. They not only helped flip the switch on the dialect cylinder implant to break the language barrier, but they were the equivalent of everything a time traveler could need. It sent vital statistics to the watchers and analysts in the Pit, where all the trackers in the agency worked together in the time travel industry.

But most important, and Sarah's favorite use, was the built-in GPS locator grid, without which they couldn't travel from point A to point B without using a time slip. It was equivalent to opening a door and stepping into another place across the street, across town, even across the country. One step would be the only thing required with a biofeed to make the journey a reality. The only drawback in Sarah's opinion was the hundreds of little probe needles attached to the biofeed band that had to slide into the user's skin.

"He's here all right," she answered, pushing the button for the second floor. "His biofeed may not be transmitting his vitals, but the idiot is posting pictures and forgot to turn off the location finder. That led me to this building. I set my biofeed to tune into the frequency emitting from the language translator. It should lead us straight to his door."

"Impressive. You'll have to teach me that trick."

She grinned. "It's a recent upgrade to the existing tech. I'll make sure you're next on the list to get one."

"So you finally hired Natalie's replacement?" Jonathan asked.

Natalie had been her right hand. She was Sarah's go-to person to get things done, and she was gone. "Natalie is irreplaceable. She was like family."

"Sarah, it's time. She isn't coming back. You have to let her go." Jonathan's look turned sincere.

Sarah sighed, not ready to let go of the notion that Natalie wasn't coming back. She'd been working at the same company since before Sarah was even adopted by her mom. Heck, Natalie had been Sarah's mother's assistant prior to her death. The woman was the epitome of knowing all and being able to anticipate everything Sarah ever needed.

Natalie had stepped in with unsolicited motherly advice when Sarah's mom died. How did they expect Sarah to replace someone as priceless as that? "I know, I just haven't had time to look through the list of suggested replacements, but I will," she assured him. "Before I forget to ask, did you ever get a chance to try out that restaurant in Paris? I heard the food is amazing."

The elevator door opened. Sarah stuck her head into the corridor and listened. No whining sound from the comm in her ear warned a translator might be on that floor. She pushed the button for the third floor as he answered. "My reservations were for tonight, but I canceled my date."

"There's still time for you to make it," she said, glancing down at her watch, mentally calculating when the Paris restaurant might close.

"I've learned not to schedule things like dates when working with you." Jonathan grinned as the elevator dinged. Sarah pointed to the translator and stepped out onto the floor.

"Did you at least reschedule?"

Jonathan rested his hand on her back and led her down the hall. "Sarah, if you believe Crenshaw is doing what you think he is, you know he will not go willingly. So bugging me about reservations and whether I eat is not on point."

"Casual conversation between friends helps decrease stress levels."

"This situation requires focus. Now do what you do best, and I'll handle the rest."

"You're avoiding the inevitable, Jonathan. You need a life," Sarah said, grabbing the hotel door handle. She pressed buttons on her biofeed; energy sizzled in her palm, dancing over her skin until she heard the click of the lock. She and Jonathan padded inside the foyer.

Marvin Crenshaw's room was dark and small. The only light came from the computer in the middle of an upload. The screen read 50% complete.

Marvin was an interesting man. When he'd arrived in 2018, his file indicated that the botanist was ahead of his time. The plant scientist had created medicines and vaccines from researching plant life in years past and taking them back to his own time of 2129 where more advanced equipment was utilized to assist in his research. This wasn't his first trip to 2018 but it was going to be his last. His plump stature had grown since his arrival. Judging from the looks of his new beer gut, he'd packed on an additional twenty pounds in the last three months.

He was steadily shoving stacks and stacks of wrapped money in his duffel bag. She flicked on the light switch, and he glanced up, pulling the earbuds from his ears. His eyes widened, and the blood drained from his face as his gaze flew from Jonathan's to hers. "Agent Weston."

"You've been a bad boy, Marvin." She smiled the way she'd perfected for all the visiting tourists. The kind that was meant to ease their worries and fears. The kind that promised that she'd handle whatever problems might crop up. She would have gotten Marvin back on the right path and helped him, if only he wouldn't have removed his biofeed and she found him sooner.

Visiting tourist was how she referred to all time traveling scientists, people visiting in Sarah's time that would eventually need to return home, similar to snowbirds in Florida. Only these tourists would travel through time instead of distance. Giving them the quaint name of tourist helped to avoid the awkward looks for anyone listening in on their conversations. These people had been visiting and popping in and out of our years in the name of research ever since Sarah was a little girl and used to visit her adoptive mom at work. This was Sarah's dream job; until now.

Marvin pulled a gun out of the duffel bag. His hand shook as he pointed at her. "Stay back, Sarah. I don't want to hurt you."

Sarah took a step, and Jonathan's hand landed on her arm. "Marvin's not going to hurt me. He knows if he does, the Magistrate would send hunters to track him down. They won't care if he gets hurt, but I care.

Marvin put down your gun and no one will have to know you threatened me."

Marvin waved the gun between Jonathan and Sarah. "Just because I don't want to hurt you doesn't mean I won't. I can't let you stop me. The world deserves to be warned and know the truth."

2

Sarah glanced at the computer, the upload now at 75%.

"Well, then we have a problem, Marvin. I briefed you on our rules when you arrived at our facility. We take those rules seriously, and you're in violation of three."

"What three?" he growled.

Sarah ticked them off on her fingers as she recited the ones he'd broken.

"No venturing into the red zone areas that can change your future, no turning your GPS tracker off. It makes it much more difficult to make sure you're safe, and under no circumstance were you to expose time travel. Breaking even one guarantees a one-way trip back home. Three? Three approves me to remove you by any means necessary. Please don't make me do that to you."

Sweat beaded on Marvin's brow. His hand holding the gun continued shaking.

"Jonathan." My partner's name was only a whisper in the quiet room when the zip of bullet left the silencer, landing in the internet modem.

Marvin's shoulders deflated as the computer transfer failed.

"Look, the choice was made for you. Come peacefully and I promise to put in a good word for you."

Marvin dropped the weapon onto the bed. A beep sounded from the backpack he'd been stuffing. Marvin grabbed for it at the same time Sarah did, and each held it pulled taut like a chew toy that neither wanted to share.

"Give it to her, Crenshaw." Jonathan's voice was calm and steady as he pointed the end of his silencer at Marvin's head.

Marvin released his hold on the bag and Sarah rested her hand on Jonathan's gun and forcing it to the ground. "Lower your weapon, Jonathan. We don't want to accidently shoot him."

"You can't stop this. The secret is going to come out." His squirrely gaze darted across the room as if looking for a way out of this predicament. He wouldn't find anywhere to hide that would prevent him from explaining his deeds to the Time Magistrate. It was the only branch of the legal system that oversaw crimes against time that forms ten years from now. Any time traveler who broke the rules were whisked in front of the court and never heard from again. The sweat on Marvin's brow dripped down his ruddy cheek.

He swiped at it with the back of his sleeve as Sarah pulled out a phone from the backpack. The message on the screen made her heart skip a beat and disappointment settle in her gut.

We've received 2 of the 3 downloads of data, please transmit again. Your other package arrived an hour ago by carrier.

"Call Nat…" Sarah's heart clenched at her slip up. "Just call Diana and have her pull an address for the text sender." Sarah tossed Jonathan the phone. No way would he make it on time to a reservation now. Their cleanup efforts had just doubled.

"You better hope I can stop whatever you've done. If you've put my friends and coworkers in danger, I'll petition the Time Magistrate to keep you stuck in this primitive time and you'll spending the rest of your life in our psych wards."

Marvin stepped back as though he could feel the danger in the air. Sarah was on the verge of snapping. If the time travelers' secrets were exposed it was dangerous for everyone involved; and that included the people Sarah held dear. Sarah held her hand behind her back and Jonathan smacked agency cuffs into her palms. She instantly slapped the cool metaled cuffs around Marvin's pudgy wrists. She punched in the calculations for the STEM Corp's holding cells.

The room sizzled to life, and a time slip opened to show the exit point was a room surrounded by iron bars. The frequency emitting from the cuffs sucked Marvin into the holding containment cell, seconds before the time slip shut.

"We've got to get in front of this and fix whatever he did," Sarah said.

"We will," Jonathan answered.

His promise did little to ease the stress that was starting to pinch at Sarah's shoulders. She and Jonathan were both in for a long night trying to unravel the mystery behind what Marvin had put into motion.

Jonathan unplugged everything from the computer's hard drive and tossed all the equipment onto the bed. He had his phone out, punching in the familiar numbers before holding the receiver to his ear. "I need a full scrub at my location."

Scrubs were no easy task. They didn't have devices like on television that could just flash away memories. Lives would be altered by the time they were done. Not that they'd kill anyone to keep their secret, even though Sarah suspected agents before her might have worked in that cowboy mentality.

Sarah headed for the door, and Jonathan covered the phone in his hand. "Diana needs to talk to you."

"Ask her if it can wait. I'm leaving now to get us

all some sushi. We're in for a long night."

Sarah pulled the door open, and an unfamiliar woman covered in blood crashed into Sarah's arms knocking them both down to the floor.

Blood from the woman's clothes stained onto Sarah's white suit. Fear covered the unknown woman's face as she moaned, still trying to struggle farther into the room and away from the white and blue lights radiating from the opened time slip in the hallway.

The time slip just outside Marvin's hotel room door remained. If Sarah hadn't been tackled, she could have just as easily stepped across the threshold into what looked to be a warehouse filled with men in the middle of a gunfight. One wrong step was all it would have taken.

Sarah's heart raced as the scene played out before her eyes. She struggled to reach her gun under the weight of the bleeding woman. Logan Cartwright, time traveler 3576, who'd arrived only six months prior, was running for the opening. The men in the distance chasing him were closing in fast. He bypassed empty wooden shelves and flinched when shots fired at him splintered the wooden shelves as he passed. All of these guys were running in the direction of the opened time slip toward Crenshaw's hotel room. Bullets whizzed by Logan and landed in the drywall near Sarah's head.

"Sarah, take cover." Jonathan yelled.

3

Sarah dragged herself and the hurt woman out of the foyer and deeper into the room seeking safety. She pressed her back against a wall providing her cover and peeked back into the foyer with her gun drawn. At the exact moment blood spurted from Logan's knee, stopping him in his tracks. She recognized the fear in his eyes.

Fear and anger clenched hold of Sarah. She'd already lost enough people she considered family in her life, no way was she losing him too. She aimed her gun at the man still charging for Logan and pulled the trigger. She clipped his arm slowing him down. More men were closing in on Logan firing shots into Crenshaw's room. Sarah lunged into the foyer emptying her clip at the intruders intending to cross the threshold and help Logan where he was struggling to stand.

"Sarah, No." Logan screamed at the same time Jonathan's arms wrapped around Sarah's waist and she was pulled back into Crenshaw's room.

"Save her and trust no one," Logan yelled as he stripped off his biofeed watch and threw it like a football player through the time slip which effectively closed the opening. Logan and the scene they'd been watching, vanished from sight, returning to the hotel's run down hallway.

Sarah's monitor flashed red as the words scrolled across the bracelet.

Logan Cartwright - Traveler 3576- vitals ceased.

Sarah struggled out of Jonathan's hold. "Why the hell did you do that? I could have saved him."

"No you couldn't."

Sarah shoved against Jonathan's chest. "You don't know that."

"Sarah, ten other men were chasing him. Killing even one might have changed time. You couldn't tell who they were with all the gunfire and smoke. What if one of them was another time traveler? Both you and Marvin would be answering to the Time Magistrate."

"They're going to kill him." Sarah screamed only stopping at the sight of the blood on her hands.

"They shot him in the knee to slow him down. If they'd wanted him dead, it would have been a head shot." Jonathan glanced down at the blood covering her hands and down the rest of her body. "Were you hit?"

Sarah shook her head. "It's not mine, it's hers."

Jonathan left Sarah's side to squat next to the unconscious woman. He eased her over and felt for a pulse. "She's still alive, although her pulse is faint. She needs medical help."

Sarah picked up Logan's biofeed meter and stared down at the blood covering the cracked glass and worn out band. "We need to find Logan and figure out what the hell is going on."

"Right now, this woman is our best shot," Jonathan said glancing up at Sarah.

"Do you know who she is?"

"No, but Logan seemed to be protecting her."

Sarah shoved loose strands of hair behind her ear. Time travelers were normally loners and for good reason. The less relationships they made, the easier it was to keep their identity and occupations a secret.

The unknown woman's red hair was matted in blood. The cuts on her pale face were shallow compared to blood soaking through her clothes. She looked as if she'd put up one hell of a fight to survive. Jonathan was right. This woman was the key Sarah needed to save Logan. No way was she dying. Sarah wouldn't let her.

"What do you want to do with her?" Jonathan asked. "Scrubbers will be here any minute, and we have to deal with Crenshaw's security leak, not to mention explaining why Logan's biofeed went offline."

Sarah glanced down at the biofeed again, running her finger over the cracked face as she debated how to handle this. Bringing an unknown person into the labs would be a defining moment. "We have to take her back to the compound and into the infirmary. We can't trust that when she wakes, she won't spill whatever she knows to the hospital staff. It's the only way."

"You're risking exposure," Jonathan said.

"She already knows about us," Sarah said letting her gaze rest on the woman's beaten body. "She used a time slip and didn't die."

Jonathan turned his gaze back to the woman. "She's not wearing a biofeed, so she's had to ingest the stabilizing agent at some point, and if that's the case, either Logan stole some of the liquid and gave it to her or she's already part of the program."

"My guess is the latter since we haven't been advised of any theft reports. Help me carry her into the infirmary."

Sarah punched in a location, and blue and white energy sizzled in the air. Jonathan picked up the woman and carried her through the time slip and inside the sterile white walls of the infirmary.

The linens on the beds were pressed and perfect. The countertops and metal surfaces shined. The sanitized room smelled like bleach.

Doctor Stillman was restocking his meds and turned when they appeared. His brows dipped as Jonathan deposited the woman on the hospital bed.

"I'll be back when the scrub is complete so we can deal with the rest of this mess," Jonathan announced.

Sarah nodded as Doc Stillman left the medicine bottles on the counter and crossed the room. He stared down at the woman while grabbing a cart full of lab utensils.

"Who is she?" Doc asked, picking up the scissors first. They looked sharp enough to cut through anything. He sliced through the wet denim fabric with ease, starting where the most blood pooled on her leg.

"I don't know, but she used a time slip. She and Logan were running for it while being shot at. Logan didn't make it."

Sarah rubbed at the blood on her hands, ignoring the pain in her chest and the rock that settled in her stomach. Her gaze washed over the woman's prone body. Recognition eluded Sarah, but whoever she was, the woman had the answers Sarah needed. Sarah cleared her throat. "Can you check her injuries while I get a status update on Logan?"

He nodded without even lifting his gaze; he continued pulling away the fabric to get to the woman's wounds. "Go. I'll treat her and let you know the minute she wakes."

"Thanks, Doctor."

Sarah stepped out of the infirmary and headed toward the command pit. She wasn't supposed to have a favorite tourist, just like parents weren't supposed to have favorite kids, but she did, and Logan was Sarah's favorite. It wasn't in a good-looking-want-to-get-him-into-bed kind of way, or even in the he's-sexy-and-smart kind of deal. No, Logan was different in a way she could only imagine as if she knew what it felt like to have an older big brother. He'd picked on her since the day he'd arrived, and she'd reciprocated in kind. The fact he'd gotten into this mess was a reminder of why she should work harder to keep relationships at a distance.

People stared at her and stepped out of her way as she made her way down the hall. She ignored the looks of confusion on their faces as she reached Diana's desk.

Diana's mouth parted as she stared back. "I thought Crenshaw was in Little China Town."

"He was."

Diana glanced down Sarah's suit. "Then why does it look like you came back from a war?"

"Oh…right." Sarah glanced down her body at the blood covering her white suit. Strands of loose hair flopped in her eyes. "I'll change later. Tell me what you know about Logan."

Diana turned her attention back to the computer and clicked buttons, pulling up Logan's biofeed readings. "He went offline, but maybe it's just another glitch." Her voice sounded hopeful.

"It wasn't a glitch." Sarah showed her Logan's biofeed. "He was shot while running for a time slip he opened at my location. I need to know everything about his GPS movements. Pull the reports for his biometer for the last month. I'm going to have Doc Stillman run DNA on the blood on the screen."

Diana slid into her chair. "You got it. Anything else?"

"Did you find out where that text for Crenshaw originated?"

"Ziggy Carmichael."

"Great. A conspiracy theorist with proof. What else can go wrong?"

Diana tried to suppress a grin and failed. "I called you earlier to warn you that Human Resources called down here to see if you've hired anyone yet for Natalie's position."

4

Sarah changed and went back to the infirmary after telling Diana to start the interruption of Ziggy's internet connection. Sarah made the mistake of passing by Human Resources. She'd just cleared the door when Mrs. Tanner popped her head out. The old lady was fast like a ninja with the interrogation skills of a Catholic schoolteacher.

"Agent Weston, we've been calling you." Mrs. Tanner raised her brow.

"I know, and I plan to pick a replacement, but now is not a good time. I've got a missing tourist and a conspiracy nut with damning proof and information. Can we do this later?"

"Putting it off won't make the situation go away." Mrs. Tanner rested a supportive hand on Sarah's arm. "Her death wasn't your fault."

"I know," Sarah said as she inched around the

Mrs. Tanner. "I promise to pick a replacement soon after I deal with all this."

"I'm holding you to that." Mrs. Tanner crossed her arms over her chest as Sarah headed down the hall.

Diana texted that she'd already frozen Ziggy's internet connection. Most people would believe a problem with the internet meant it stemmed with their service provider, and sometimes it did. But in the cases with time travelers, it was Sarah's agency making the computers glitch and seize up while her group formed plans to contain and undo the damage.

Keeping secrets was an issue even scientists couldn't prevent. One pair of loose lips tells another one, and then a chain reaction ensues, even without proof, spawning a new revolution of believers jumping on board. That was how the public started fantasizing about time travelers. A few real videos that slipped by, along with the fake ones, and it always drew more interest in something that many had already forgotten.

When the company was ever on the verge of being discovered, they created diversions. A news piece that turned attention elsewhere. It didn't happen often, but the one time it did, the Roswell weather balloon was invented. And it worked like a charm, shifting suspicions from time travelers to aliens. Their sister agency was still holding the grudge.

Sarah opened the door to the infirmary and paused

at the scene playing out before her eyes. Doc Stillman had a needle in his hands with his thumb on the plunger, ready to press, as he was trying to get closer to the unknown woman. The woman had backed herself into a corner, holding a metal tray in front of her.

"What are you doing, Doc?" Sarah asked.

"I was trying to get her into a hospital gown, and she woke up and attacked me. I'm trying to give her something to calm her down."

The bed sheet lay strewn on the floor. The woman stood in her bra and panties with a bandage taped to her side that was seeping blood.

"You try." Doc Stillman tossed a hospital gown and the pair of scrubs at Sarah.

She led the woman into the bathroom and held up the shirt to prove she wasn't trying anything funny. "What's your name?"

She didn't answer. Her entire body shivered, and she had a wild gleam in her eyes as if scared Sarah or Doc Stillman might be a bad guy like the ones that had chased her. Sarah helped dress her and tried again for information.

"My name is Sarah. You're safe here. Logan and I were friends."

"Logan," the woman whispered.

"Yes, how do you know Logan?" Sarah asked.

"Logan," the woman repeated. Her wide glassy eyes remained unfocused.

"It's okay. You're safe, and we'll find Logan." Sarah ushered the dressed woman out of the bathroom and almost back onto the hospital bed.

"Logan," the girl repeated and hurried to her tattered jeans on the table. She scoured through her pockets and pulled out a folded piece of paper and handed it to Sarah. "Logan." Determination filled her voice unlike the crazed woman from moments ago.

Sarah unfolded the paper, and her brows dipped at the name scribbled inside. "Dr. Claremont."

"Retired before your time and be glad. He was a cantankerous stubborn ass to deal with," Dr. Stillman said as he poured the woman some water.

The door opened, and Jonathan poked his head inside. "Sarah, can I see you…"

"Just a sec." Sarah watched as the woman drank water from the plastic cup. She'd finished the entire contents before she put the cup back down. Sarah picked up the empty glass with a pair of latex gloves and poured her some more water into another cup and slid it in front of the woman.

The woman's face remained stoic.

Sarah shook open a plastic medical bag reserved for personal belongings and slid the plastic cup inside. "I'll be back. You're safe here."

She turned to leave, with the doctor following her to the door. "She's the key to us finding Logan, and he thought she was in danger. Keep the lid on her situation until I figure things out."

"I'm going to have to report her. You took a risk bringing her here."

"Doc, we both know that analysts and time travelers alike are given a stabilizing agent before working here or arriving in the transponder room. They're giving the stabilizing agent to survive walking through a time slip. This woman not only walked through a time slip, but she survived, so unless someone is missing some stabilizing agent in inventory, then I have more questions than answers." Sarah glanced at the bloody clothes. "Do you think you can run some DNA on her clothes?"

"Of course," he said, gesturing to the cart where Logan's biofeed lay. "I'll also run a sample of the blood found on Logan's biofeed. You have until I get the results back and then I have to report her to Dr. Bay. He needs to know he has a threat in the building."

"I'll inform him after I figure out who she is." Sarah lifted the cup. "I should know who she is after I send her prints through the database."

Sarah stepped out of the room to find Jonathan pacing in the hall and running his hand through his disheveled hair. "What's with the cup?"

"The woman's fingerprints."

"Smart," he said. "We have a problem."

"Only one, Jonathan?" Sarah asked. "Scrubber's finished?"

"Yeah, and I visited our favorite little internet

conspiracy theorist," he said, pulling Sarah into one of the briefing rooms. He shut the door and lowered the blinds.

"What's wrong?"

"Sarah, Ziggy had a ton of emails from Crenshaw."

Sarah's eyes widened. "Did you wipe them?"

"I didn't have a chance. I almost got caught in his room, but I made a copy of Ziggy's hard drive so we'll know what we're dealing with." Jonathan held up a thumb drive. "Sarah, your name was in some of the documents. We need to deal with this before it gets out of control."

5

"Let's run the prints first and see who this woman is." Sarah slipped the thumb drive out of his hand and headed toward the basement tech lab with Jonathan following her. Everything in Sarah's life was on the verge of collapsing around her. Marvin was one of her assigned tourist, and she still didn't know what damage he'd created for her to clean up. Logan, well…he was like family, and now Sarah had broken the company protocols by bringing an unauthorized person onto Lab property. She needed more than answers. She wanted her sanity back.

Sarah and Jonathan entered the lab, and Ritter didn't even skip a beat in his project, somehow knowing it was them. Ritter, the red-headed Irish recruit, was the company tech guy. His horn-rimmed glasses were perched on his forehead as he peered through a large magnifying glass down at one of the biofeed's electrical circuits. Ritter was a genius, merging science with mechanics and tech. He was Sarah's resident go-to guy, and it had been Ritter's idea on how to find Crenshaw. He was gifted beyond his time.

"If you came down here to yell, don't bother. I still haven't figured out what the heck is making these biofeeds glitch, and I'm knee deep in figuring it out. Sarah, yours is the worst. Each one I give you keeps screwing up. It's as if you've got your own electrical current that keeps throwing it offline."

"That's not why we're here," Sarah said, resting her palm over her biofeed.

"If you came to tell me my invention helped you nab Crenshaw, I already know."

Sarah exchanged a look with Jonathan. Obviously, the news hadn't traveled down into the basement where Ritter liked to work.

"You haven't heard?" Sarah asked.

Ritter lifted his gaze, his tools frozen in mid-air. "I hear everything, including the fact that you still haven't picked a replacement for the assistant position."

"Forget the assistant. Natalie is irreplaceable. That's not why we're here. This is more important."

Ritter's brows dipped in question.

"Logan's biofeed went offline," Sarah said.

"Is he here? Tell him to come down, and I'll

assign him a new one." Ritter sighed and laid his tools down.

Poor guy. This would hit him hard. Ritter had looked up to Logan and vice versa. Logan had way of making friends with people in the agency and a few people outside of it. Relationships were to be limited with people outside the agency. Time travelers had to be extremely careful about their existence and the proof left behind. That's why Sarah's job was so important. But Logan was charismatic and just an all-around good guy and a great scientist.

Logan wasn't a recluse like many that had came through the program. Their friendship complemented each other's weaknesses. Where Logan excelled in the field, it was only because Ritter's inventions had helped him flourish.

Sarah crossed the room and rested her hand on Ritter's arm. "His biofeed went offline because he took it off while being shot at."

"I don't understand. Is he upstairs in the infirmary?"

"We don't know where he is," Sarah said.

"If he's not upstairs being treated and you know he was being shot at… are you telling me he's dead?" Ritter's brows furrowed.

"I'm not sure, but we saw it happen. Somehow he tapped into the GPS in my biofeed. He opened a time slip to my location and sent a woman through, telling us to protect her. He took his watch and tossed it inside the time slip opening so the shooters couldn't follow the woman. Before the slip closed, guys with guns were closing in on Logan. We couldn't help him. We tried." Sarah ignored her clenching gut. If Jonathan hadn't stopped her she could have helped him. She should have done something more. Something… anything.

"What woman? He didn't tell me he was seeing anyone," Ritter said, narrowing his eyes. "He hasn't told me about any assignments. Logan was about to be on vacation. I saw him two weeks ago, and before you even suggest it, no way did he share company secrets with an outsider. Just don't," Ritter growled. The muscles in his arms flexed each time he created a fist and released it. Sarah could read the signs Ritter was fighting his need to help and on the verge of leaving his lab.

Sarah dangled the medical bag with the cup. "I was hoping you could run her fingerprints while we're waiting on her DNA. We need to know who she is and her prints are on the cup."

"Absolutely," he said, taking the cup.

Sarah watched as he pulled the prints and ran them through the computer connected to every known three-letter agency known to man, including the secret mainframes like the lab's.

Within minutes the computer dinged.

Ritter read the result. "Emma Stanton- TT 267-File Classified." Ritter gawked as if the words were a foreign language he didn't comprehend. His fingers flew quicker across the keyboard. "Classified? I've got top clearance."

It flashed classified again, and Sarah moved him out of the way and typed in her log-in access codes. She had access to the quantum computer. Sarah's had better work.

"Emma Stanton- TT 267- File Classified." Sarah frowned. She'd never had information withheld from her. Ever. She typed in a few more commands, unmasking who'd designated the files as classified.

"Dr. Richard Bay," she said, rising from Ritter's seat. It made sense. The CEO of the company had a higher clearance than any of them. The only question left was, why was there a traveler that she hadn't been informed she should be watching?

She headed for the door and yanked it open with Jonathan following her. "Do you think you can convince him into declassifying the file?"

"Actually, I do." Sarah punched the elevator button in quick succession. The elevator dinged, and the doors slid open. Jonathan followed her inside as she hit the button for the top executive floors.

"You need to tread carefully, Sarah," Jonathan said.

His words went in one ear and right out the other. If whatever Richard the Dick had deemed classified kept her from doing her job, she refused to pussyfoot around the conversation.

The doors opened, and the atmosphere was different from the basement where Ritter worked. The light streamed in through the floor-to-ceiling windows. It was a happier vibe, like these people didn't have a care in the world while sitting in their ivory tower. Strategically placed art pieces and expensive seating bordered the waiting room.

Jonathan and Sarah strolled up to Dr. Bay's receptionist, and Sarah smiled down at her. "Carol, I need to see Richard, please. It's urgent."

"Sarah, if you'll please have a seat. He's in another meeting, but I can fit you in afterward."

"It can't wait, Carol." Sarah stepped around Carol's desk and headed down the hallway. The hurried tapping of Carol's heels as she chased after Sarah wouldn't stop her from entering Richard's office.

Jonathan's smooth sexy voice carried down the hallway. "Carol, I thought maybe we could get a drink."

"Move it, Jonathan. If she goes in there, I'll be in trouble."

"Did you cut your hair? It looks good on you." Jonathan continued.

Sarah glanced over her shoulder and grinned as Jonathan moved from side to side in the hallway blocking Carol's path with his flirtatious ways.

Sarah pushed Dr. Bay's door open to find he'd been meeting with the Deputy Director of the FBI,

Eleonore Myers. Both the doctor and the director were reading something in files stamped classified.

Richard rose from his desk. "Agent Weston, have you lost your mind?"

"It's okay, Richard. Our meeting was almost over." Eleonore rose and crossed the room, meeting Sarah halfway. Her styled hair sat in a tight bun at the back of her head. The bun was tighter than Sarah's, but that wasn't the main difference between Sarah and Eleonore. It was their suits. Where Sarah liked to wear white, Eleonore was always in the standard-issue black. "Agent Weston, I've heard wonderful things about you."

"Thank you, Deputy Director. I apologize for barging in," Sarah lied, ignoring the heat claiming her cheeks.

"You can call me, Eleonore, dear." She patted Sarah's hand in passing and paused outside the door where Jonathan was smiling like an idiot for a job well done.

"And you must be Jonathan. They told me wherever Sarah went you would always be close behind."

"Yes, ma'am," Jonathan answered without looking away.

"We're partners," Sarah scoffed.

"Of course." Eleonore winked as she pulled the doors closed behind her.

"You better have a good reason for barging in,

Sarah, before I strip you of the head analyst title and move you down to cleaning toilets."

Sarah lifted her chin and slid her hands into her pockets, refusing to be intimidated by the threat of a demotion. "Emma Stanton- TT 267."

He paused in shutting the file. His look turned from one of annoyance to uncertainty. "Where did you hear that name?"

"Sir, I need to know everything there is to know about her."

Doctor Bay slid into his seat and had a look on his face that indicated his world suddenly made little sense. He steepled his fingers together. "I haven't heard that name in a long time."

"Sir, please. I wouldn't be up here if it weren't important. Logan Cartwright opened a time slip to my location and sent a woman through. He was being shot at by men chasing him. His very life could depend on learning everything we can about this woman. Please, sir, tell me what you know."

Richard sat forward and rubbed his hands up and down his face. "As you know time travel has been going on for years. But five years ago, eight women arrived in the year 2013, including the woman we referred to as Emma Stanton."

"Why were they hiding for the last five years?" Sarah asked.

"Witness protection program," he answered.

"What time period are they from?"

"We have no idea what time frame they came from. They kept that a secret to help hide the women's identities. Their records were erased years ago, and other than their new associated IDs with their real names and fingerprints, their files were closed as classified."

"What were they witness to?" she asked.

Dr. Bay rubbed his neck. "I'm not sure, but the fact they needed to send these woman to a different time period, just to keep them safe, told my mother everything she needed to know at the time. She kept the information from even myself. I just know their names and they're here and in hiding."

Sarah's mouth parted. "You're telling me that your mother, the former CEO of this organization, helped to hide seven other travelers here, besides Emma, and we haven't been tracking any of them?"

"More than that. Each witness had a handler with them. When they arrived and with the help of the FBI, my mother gave them new identities, a new life, new jobs, everything they needed to live in safety."

"You're saying that there are *sixteen* other people in this time period that don't belong?" Sarah rose from her seat, and anger stirred through her throbbing veins as a piercing headache started to form. How in the hell had they been able to keep this secret for so long?

"Fourteen," he corrected. "I'm sorry, Sarah, but

Emma and her handler died in the car crash with your adoptive mom."

The woman that raised Sarah was the whole reason she knew time travel existed. It was because of her work as a scientist and analyst at STEM Corp, Sarah had been given a job. The people in the company had all watched Sarah grow up.

Sarah rested her hand to calm the unease in her stomach. No one had ever told her they believed there were more passengers in her mother's car. Sarah was supposed to have been with her that day. Sarah should have been driving on their trip.

"Emma is alive. No one else was in the car with my mother. I've read the report."

"The FBI omitted some things from the report that linked back to this agency. Emma died with your mom. Authorities flagged her identity and her handler's when they worked the accident. Everyone was announced DOA."

"Emma is not only alive, but she's downstairs in the infirmary. Where do you think I got her prints?"

6

Sarah, Jonathan, and Dr. Richard Bay looked on from the observation room at Emma Stanton lying in the infirmary bed.

"Is that the woman they declared dead?" Sarah asked.

Dr. Bay rubbed the stubble on his chin. "I don't know, Sarah. She looks like her, but there's something different."

"The prints don't lie. Is it possible the files got mixed up? How can we get our hands on the original files?"

Dr. Bay turned to face Sarah. "You don't understand. They didn't come with entire files. They placed these women in the witness protection program. Only their handlers know why."

"So your predecessors let them in on good faith?" Sarah asked.

"Neither my mother or I had a choice. The FBI and I complied with orders from the quantum computer," Richard answered. "Has she said anything?"

"No, if anyone would know what's going on besides her, it's Logan."

"If he isn't already dead," Jonathan added.

"Has the retrieval team come back from Logan's last GPS transmitted coordinates?" Sarah asked.

"There was no sign of him except blood in that abandoned warehouse. Diana is pulling street cams from the vicinity. We should have more answers by morning."

By morning. Sarah sighed. They were wasting time they didn't have. She had to find Dr. Claremont to figure out why Emma had his name, and she needed to find Logan, hopefully still alive. She needed to look at the emails Marvin had sent to the conspiracy theorist and devise a way to make them disappear, and she still had to figure out what other trouble Marvin had planned.

Sarah's day was ending in a complete 180 degrees of where it started.

"What are we going to do about her?" Sarah asked. "Logan said to protect her, but we have no idea what we're protecting her from."

"She'll be fine here overnight. Doctor Stillman and his staff can keep an eye on her. We'll let him know to be vigilant, and no one enters without using their biofeed. We'll heighten security protocols and make the infirmary self-contained." Dr. Bay spun on his heels. "Get some rest, Sarah. You're going to need it for tomorrow to sort through this mess."

Sarah ignored Dr. Bay as he walked away, pulling out his cell phone and dialing digits. They should have all known that keeping this type of information from the analyst would end up in a situation just like this.

7

She'd dug through the emails Ziggy had on his computer. There was the promise of future evidence and more names forthcoming. Promises of how to bypass the protocols along with the facilities locations and instructions on how to work a biofeed. Even the promise of a secret that Crenshaw claimed to know that the rest of them didn't.

Even if Ziggy had figured out the biofeed, without drinking the stabilizing agent like the rest of STEM Corps employees and the time traveling scientists, he would have died if he'd tried to venture through a time slip. Crenshaw did more damage than just offering company secrets. He hadn't bothered to warn the conspiracy nut that it could kill him if he ever tried to maneuver with the biofeed. There would be one more death on Sarah's resume for not being able to stop it. It was two a.m. as she struggled to keep her eyes open and continue to work. She'd fallen asleep in her chair with the laptop on her lap. Hours later she went to her room and quickly fell asleep. It seemed like she'd just closed her eyes when her alarm blared, waking her out of her slumber.

The sun hadn't even risen yet. It was the time she woke up every day. Every day she had the same routine. A run on her favorite beach before she greeted the day. It helped calm her mind and center herself, and if there was ever a day she needed it, today was that day.

Sarah sent an urgent text to Dr. Bay, asking him to take Ritter and Diana with him to check in with Eleonore at the FBI to see if they could possibly track some files on these tourists that didn't belong. She wanted to jump right in with the information when she returned.

She stared at her cellphone in relief when he replied they'd be leaving for the FBI by seven to get an early start.

Sarah changed into her jogging clothes and stepped through a time slip, re-emerging straight from her onsite living quarters and into her beach house. She hit the back porch steps with a jog and inhaled the salty breeze as she ran.

Sarah Weston's breath came in quick pants as her feet pounded the packed sand near the shoreline. Breaking waves crested and barreled closer to the shore with every step. Heavy fog blanketed the salty air clinging to her clothes and mixing with her sweat. Her lungs burned. The memories of the fear in Logan's face flashed in her mind with each jarring movement. Sarah ran to drown similar haunting memories. She ran to forget. She'd run forever.

The sun crested the horizon, and with it came the promise of another day.

Sarah left the ease of the packed sand. Her shoes sunk deeper into the famous sugary white sands Florida's Gulf Coast was known for. Her calves strained while she ran through the soft grains making her way toward the wooden stairs of her beach house. She ran her fingers along the worn wood railing as she reached the top and turned back to jog down and climb up them again. Her fingers came away wrapped in the spindles of a thin spider web.

The pounding of her heart against her ribs slowed with each deep breath. She grabbed her towel from the nearby chair and ran it over her soaked hair and down the salt clinging to her skin. Jonathan was on her porch, lounging in one of her lawn chairs.

"Well, this is a nice surprise," Sarah said, plopping down opposite him, trying to catch her breath. "You must be eager to start the day."

Jonathan handed her a water bottle and frowned as he met Sarah's gaze. He swung his legs over the chair and put them firmly on the ground. "You've been gone from the compound for what an hour? Maybe two?"

All the tension in her shoulders that she'd just gotten rid of during her run was returning. She could feel the trouble brewing in her bones. She glanced at her watch. "Close to two, why?"

"I don't know how to tell you this, but there's been a situation."

Dread slithered through Sarah's veins. "I sent Diana and Ritter to the FBI. Did something happen to them?"

He shook his head. "No, you probably saved their lives. Diana and Ritter are safe. They were off-site with Dr. Bay and Eleonore trying to find locations and names on the other witness protection people."

"Okay." Relief flooded her body. "What happened?" Sarah asked, rising and setting the coordinates into her biofeed for a slip to open and take her back to the Pit.

He rested his hand over her fingers, stopping her from completing the sequence. "You can't return, or you'll walk into firemen trying to put out flames. They damaged the facility, Sarah."

"Who did, and what kind of damage are you talking about?" she growled.

"I don't know yet. Judging from the impact and damage, I'd venture a guess it was some type of bomb or experiment gone wrong. No one knows yet for sure."

Sarah covered her mouth with her hand. "Casualties?"

"Several. Those that survived but got hurt are being taken to County General for treatment. Those with insignificant scratches and abrasions are being handled on-site. The FBI is running point on the incident."

Jonathan pulled her into his arms and hugged her. "I couldn't find you. I thought I'd lost you."

She rested in his strength, stealing a minute in time for just herself to process the ramifications on what awaited her return.

"I always run at six in the morning," she whispered.

"Diana told me," he said, resting his chin on top of her head.

"What about Emma Stanton, Doc Stillman?" Sarah asked, leaning out of his grasp to search the answer in his eyes.

"The infirmary was near the labs. That part of the building had the most damage. But we won't know until we can get in for a better assessment. We can only hope the transponder room isn't a complete wash."

"Oh my God, how many people are trapped?" she asked, realizing the extent of what this meant.

There were potentially more casualties, and if the transponder room was gone, the tourists were stuck on a permanent vacation. The only good news was that time slips worked independent of the transponder room. It used the same technology but wasn't reliant on the transponder room. They just used the same type of energy to make things work and that energy was harnessed into the biofeed watches.

"And Marvin Crenshaw? He was in the holding facility," Sarah said.

Jonathan shrugged. "I don't know yet."

"Has anyone warned the tourists they may be trapped here?" Sarah asked.

"Diana sent out an emergency distress signal for all of them to meet at Area 2 and to await further information. Diana, Ritter, and Dr. Bay are waiting on you to show up so you two can explain what's going on."

"I don't know what the hell is going on. What am I supposed to say?" Sarah growled.

Jonathan rested his warm palms on her arms. "You're the problem solver, not me, but I have faith you'll solve this one."

"And where are you going?" she asked Jonathan as he punched coordinates into his biofeed.

"To the hospital, to better assess the situation and see who ended up hurt. I believe the FBI has already leaked that it was an experiment gone wrong to use as a cover."

Sarah stared up into Jonathan's eyes. "What if this is related to Emma and Logan? Or what if this was part of Crenshaw's master plan to expose us?"

"He'll be the first one I'm looking for at the hospital. If he's breathing, I'll get him to talk."

8

Sarah didn't even shower before hurrying inside and grabbing a STEM Corporation jacket. Her baseball cap, yoga pants, and a sweaty tank top would have to do until she had time to make herself presentable.

She stepped through the time slip into Area 2. The site housed all the company's vehicles, including a jet. It was on the property but away from the main building. This place was their rally point. In case of an emergency, the agency would transform Area 2 into command central.

Voices echoed off the vaulted steel walls. Blankets were being pulled out of storage and wrapped around some workers from the lab building, the lucky ones who had survived and escaped.

Some doctors and lab professors were attending to the wounded along with the other time travelers that had arrived. The camaraderie showed humanity at its finest. A side the world would never see. Generations of people coming together to help one another. It stole her breath and humbled her. This was what mattered.

Sarah spotted Diana filling a coffee cup, and she headed in her direction. Diana held it out to her side as Sarah approached while filling the next one.

"You couldn't know it was me."

"Like clockwork," Diana said, turning to face Sarah. "For a minute I thought you might be smack-dab in the middle of it considering the blast was near your room, but then all I had to do was look at the clock to know you were nowhere close."

"Thank God for my OCD tendencies," Sarah teased. "So what do we know?"

"Several people had mentioned a power outage before the explosion occurred. The guards in the holding center said they got everyone out and are keeping them detained.

"Crenshaw?" Sarah asked.

"Yep. I figured you might want to talk to him."

"What about Emma Stanton and the infirmary?" Sarah asked.

Diana swallowed, taking a tentative breath. "Total loss to that area with expected fatalities."

Sarah's mouth parted as words escaped her, making her momentarily speechless. She shook her head in disbelief. Logan had risked his life to get Emma into Sarah's custody, and now she'd lost them both? Sarah clenched her eyes closed and lowered her head.

"I've got to find the answers to who the hell that woman is and what she's doing hiding in our time line. So what are we working with?"

"I can work with the few old computers until we get clearance for the building. Ritter has the biofeed graveyard for parts and pieces until he gets clearance to check out the basement, but we don't have any idea what's going on with the transponder room. Whatever everyone has on them and what we have in storage is all we have until we know for sure what got damaged."

"What about the quantum computer room?"

"It was equipped to withstand a direct hit, and the room was state-of-the art. If fire remotely found a way in, the ventilation system would suck all the air out of the room."

"Thank God for that."

Diana held out a gun and a pair of handcuffs to Sarah. "If you're going to find answers, you may need these. You know, if you'd go ahead and pick an assistant, then she could make sure you have all the toys you need to do your job and not me."

"Why would I do that when you already know me so well?"

Diana rolled her eyes as Sarah stuffed both the handcuffs and gun in the waistband of her yoga pants then pulled her T-shirt over to cover them.

"I've done a head count of the travelers. Everyone is accounted for besides Logan and that woman, although there are a handful of employees I believe are missing."

There was an ominous feeling in the air as Dr. Bay stood on a chair and whistled trying to get everyone's attention. His gaze traveled around the room. "As you can tell, we've experienced a setback. At this time we're unsure what caused the explosion, and we're doing everything we can to control the situation."

Diana and Sarah exchanged a look that indicated they knew all of their weekend plans for the next year were now on hold to help in the rebuild. Dr. Bay bypassed Sarah's gaze as if he knew she understood the meaning behind his words. It was because she did.

"If there is any damage to the transponder room, rest assured that we have the confidential plans to rebuild the program to send everyone home. Until then, all activities are to resume as normal, but each traveler has to be more vigilant about exposure."

Sarah wouldn't have sent any of them back out into the field to continue their research, but that decision wasn't up to her. Dr. Bay ran this circus. Sarah was only responsible for the flying monkeys.

There were questions and answers for Sarah and Dr. Bay, but none of the hard ones came until Deputy Director Eleonore Myers showed up. She stood at the hangar entrance and met Sarah's and Dr.

Bay's gaze. She pointed at each and then tilted her head.

Sarah and Dr. Bay stepped out of the hanger to find Eleonore waiting with her arms crossed. "Preliminary reports show this wasn't an accident."

Sarah exchanged a worried look with Richard. "Why would you say that?"

"Someone cut the electricity from the power grid station in the north field before the explosion inside. We're dusting for prints. We'll run them, but if it's one of your guys, then they might not be in our system."

"Have they pulled any bodies from the infirmary?"

"No bodies were recovered, but they're still sorting through that area. There was a ton of damage."

"But there could be bodies?"

"Let me rephrase that. Only half the infirmary went up in flames. There was a ton of damage before the sprinklers in that area helped to extinguish them. There were no bodies to discover in that location."

I glanced at Richard. "Someone got to Emma and Dr. Stillman."

"You're looking at more than one person. You're looking for a team. At least one in the north field dealing with the power and the other on the inside considering the fire and the explosion occurred on the opposite side of the building," Eleonore said.

"You're assuming that one would need to walk or even run to accomplish both." Sarah raised her arm and pointed to her biofeed. "The laws of physics don't apply to us. One person could have done both."

"They would have had to catch Dr. Stillman off guard and knocked him unconscious. He would have fought," Dr. Bay said.

"Unless he knew his attacker. We're looking for someone who has been in the infirmary in order for it to open up to the exact location and for it to have been just one person. Any other GPS coordinates and they would have been seen elsewhere in the building."

"This was a well thought out plan."

"Regardless of whether it's one or two people," Richard said, "how are you going to track Emma if she doesn't have a biofeed and most of our equipment is off-limits?"

"When I brought Emma in, all she would say was Logan's name, but she gave me a slip of paper with another name on it; an old employee. I only need some way of finding him."

"What's the name?" Eleonore asked.

"Dr. Claremont," Sarah answered.

Within minutes Eleonore sent the address, GPS coordinates, and property layout to Sarah's phone. The address wasn't one she could just pop into due to all the security cameras and guards at the location. "Thanks, keep me apprised if they discover anything else with the fire and explosion."

As Sarah walked off, Dr. Bay appeared by her side. "Maybe I should go with you."

"Why would you want to?" Sarah asked.

"Grumpy doctors and scientists who think they're the smartest men in the room can be difficult."

Sarah's lips twitched. Dr. Richard "Dick" Bay was describing himself, and Sarah had years of experience handling him. "I think I can manage. You've got your hands full here."

"Where is he located?"

"His house straddles the country borders; half inside the US and other half over the Canadian line. I'm guessing he did it to be strategic."

It couldn't be for tax purposes. The thought of having to pay and submit taxes in both countries sent a shiver down Sarah's spine. The cameras and the border patrols alone would keep anyone from showing up unwanted unless familiar with the GPS coordinates and the exact layout of Dr. Claremont's home.

Sarah punched the coordinates to one of the safe houses in the hills of upstate New York. She opened the portal and had just stepped into it when an explosion rocked the cabin, sending her flying back into the time slip and onto her butt in front of the Dr. Bay and Eleonore.

Dr. Bay and Eleonore were quick to her side, helping Sarah sit up. "What the hell was that?"

"Our safe house has been compromised." Sarah

stared up at Richard as anger and determination raged through her veins. "You need to keep all the scientists here while we send out scouts to check the other locations."

"Give me the addresses, and I'll send out teams to inspect each one," Eleonore offered.

Dr. Bay and Sarah shared a look. "We can't. If we did, then all our sites could be compromised."

"I'm not some damn terrorist. I'm the Deputy Director of the FBI."

"And we aren't just scientists trying to win a contest at the state fair. Right now those safe houses are all we have left, and if you send out the addresses to your teams, who's to say one of your agents wouldn't give up our secrets for the right amount of money?" Dr. Bay shook his head vehemently.

"While you two argue about that, I'm going to try another safe house," Sarah said, pushing to her feet. She typed more GPS coordinates into her biofeed and awaited the opening. She eased over the threshold and peered around.

9

Sarah cautiously stepped into the new location at the safe house in upstate New York. It was the closest place to pop into that was near the border. The time slip closed behind her. She stood in place and watched the dust moats float on the air from the sun streaming into the cabin from the partially closed blinds.

She opened her ears. No ticking clocks, no voices, nothing but silence and the birds chirping nearby.

The log cabin was in the middle of nowhere, a little getaway from the world and used to research wilderness habitats and life forms from the trees to the animals roaming among them.

Few travelers lived in seclusion with the way they were wired. Studying everything around them included the culture. And the woods lacked culture. It was one of the reasons Sarah was familiar with the location of this particular cabin and the nearby lake.

The solitude was something she severely lacked, even at her beach house, where hordes of spring-breakers and visiting families during the summer months clogged her views.

A blue-and-forest-green plaid throw hung over the back of the couch. The air was stale, and if Sarah had more time, she might air out the place. Time was something she lacked, ironic considering the field she worked in.

No dishes lay in the sink, and judging by the food in the cabinets, it looked as though no one had used the place since the last time crews had stocked the kitchen. She opened the fridge to find the bottle of wine she and Jonathan had left last time they'd used the location.

They'd almost thrown caution to the wind and given into their primal instincts. It was a relationship doomed from the start. It was in this exact location she'd learned the fate of her adoptive mom in that fatal car crash. Sarah should have been with her that night. Instead she'd backed out of those plans in favor of spending time with Jonathan. Their relationship had never gotten off the ground.

She learned a lot about herself that night. That had been the last time Sarah let herself dream of anything more than the job.

A board from the porch creaked making her pause

in place. The sound of someone turning the door handle escalated her heart rate. She could handle herself against danger. The company and her adoptive mom had seen to that. Her years of martial arts and learning how to street fight would serve her well if it wasn't a bear looking to get inside in search of honey. Sarah grabbed the bottle of wine and gripped it by the neck, hurrying to move behind the opening door ready to bash the bottle over the intruders head. This weapon was less lethal and much quieter should there be more than one intruder.

The door slowly creaked opened, but the intruder didn't step inside.

"Sarah Weston. I know you're in there." She didn't recognize the man's voice, so she remained quiet. Only Dr. Bay and Eleonore knew where she was going, and with the system down, no one could even track her whereabouts by her biofeed.

"We have a common goal. Dr. Claremont. You're seeking him, and I'm protecting him."

Sarah stepped around the door, putting a face to the voice.

His brown hair was styled straight out of a magazine with a designer suit to match. His dark blue eyes held a mystery. His jaw ticked as he stared down at her. "Sarah Weston?"

"Who's asking?"

He sighed in that way that Sarah brought out in all the men in her life. "Foster."

"Foster who?" she asked.

"Just Foster," he said. "So are we doing this on the porch, or are you inviting me in?"

Sarah stepped out onto the porch, unwilling to put down her wine bottle. The thick green glass could do some serious damage.

"Okay then," Foster said, stepping off the porch and back into the yard.

He was smart to stay out of reach. Smart enough that she noticed him remove his hands from his pocket as if expecting trouble.

"Why are you protecting Dr. Claremont?"

"Why are you looking for him?" he asked.

"How do you know I'm looking for him?"

Foster's lips twitched. "The same way I knew I would find you here. Your turn. Tell me what you want."

"I need information that only he can give me."

Foster slid his hands into his pockets and tilted his head. "STEM Corporation has all of his old work. There's nothing he knows that isn't documented."

"I might have believed that two days ago," she said. "But you're wrong. He knows sensitive classified data."

Foster raised a brow. "And what qualifies you to be privy to this classified information?"

"Someone tried to destroy STEM Corporation today while I had an unsanctioned jumper in the building. Someone only he can tell me more about."

"Someone tried to destroy the lab?" he asked while rubbing his neck. "Why?"

"If I knew, I wouldn't be here. I think it had to do with the unsanctioned woman that had a slip of paper with Claremont's name written on it."

"Now I know you're lying. Claremont would never break protocol. He's a stickler for the rules."

"Yeah, well. Wrong again. Maybe you don't know Claremont at all."

Foster's eye twitched as if she'd hit a nerve. "Who's the woman, and what program was she in?"

"Emma Stanton and the program she's in is classified. Have you not heard a word I just said?"

"I've heard every word. You know what word won't get you within two feet of the doctor? Classified." He grinned. "I'm afraid I need more."

"I didn't ask for an escort to meet the doctor. I'm extremely capable of finding him myself."

A hint of humor passed Foster's eyes, and she almost missed it. He slid his sleeve up his arm. He had a biofeed similar to Sarah's, only a slightly different design. "I'll see if he'll agree."

His gaze slid down to her yoga pants. "I see they got rid of the dress code at STEM Corporation."

"I'm sure they don't care what the hell I'm wearing right now while I get this sorted out."

His lips twitched. "Give me a couple hours to convince the old man to talk to you."

Sarah stepped off the porch, leaving the bottle on

the railing, and approached the man. She slipped cuffs from beneath her shirt and held them behind her back. She lifted her hand to shake his. When he shook it, she slapped one handcuff over his wrist and the other on her own. "I'm sorry, but we don't have time to waste. There are lives at stake."

10

His eyes narrowed at her only seconds before his lips twisted into a smile. "After meeting him, you may wish you hadn't done that."

"I'm pretty sure you're wrong."

Foster pushed a button on his biofeed and picked her up around the waist with the hand that wasn't cuffed, squishing their linked hands between their bodies. Electricity sizzled between them. He stared deep into Sarah's eyes as if trying to read her soul as he stepped through the slip, leaving the greenery of the forest behind. They arrived in a cluttered warehouse.

The warehouse looked as though a hermit lived there. There were stacks of books and papers covering the tables and shelves. Whiteboards and chalkboards lined the walls with equations written over each. None made sense to her.

The air was considerably colder, and she shivered in Foster's arms. His gaze searched hers, for what she wasn't sure.

"You brought her here? Have you lost your damn mind?" an older voice croaked from across the room.

Foster lowered Sarah to her feet and lifted his arm with the handcuffs. "Sorry, Dr. Claremont, she didn't leave me a choice."

Dr. Claremont's brows dipped for mere seconds before he pasted a smile on his face. "That's more inventive than the stories I've been told about you, Ms. Weston."

"You've heard of me? How? Are you still in contact with some people at the lab?"

"You aren't the first to seek me out," Dr. Claremont answered.

"Who else came looking? Emma Stanton?" Sarah asked.

Dr. Claremont climbed down from the podium where he was working on some type of scientific project that Sarah couldn't identify.

"No, not Emma," he said, walking across the room. He started down a hall. "Come along."

Sarah exchanged a look with Foster when he punched in a sequence on the handcuffs and they unlatched from both of their wrists. He caught the shackles before they dropped to the ground. He dangled them in front of her and smiled. "They all come equipped with the emergency release code 999.

Come on, he doesn't like to be kept waiting, and it's time for him to eat lunch and to take his pills." He leaned in to whisper in Sarah's ear. "He gets cranky if he doesn't get his dessert, and he doesn't get his dessert unless he takes his pills."

Sarah followed behind Foster down the hall, unsure she trusted him enough to give him her back.

They climbed a flight of stairs, and Foster stepped out into a hallway, holding the door open for Sarah. "He's fond of you, Agent Weston."

"And how again has he heard about me?"

Foster turned to block the entrance into a living room. "Maybe one day he'll tell you. When he does, that's when you'll know he trusts you."

"What's your story?" Sarah asked, following him through the living room toward another door. "Why are you playing babysitter to a retired scientist?"

Foster's lips twisted. "Whoever said he retired?"

"Are you two going to get in here, or are you going to make me eat by myself?"

Foster stepped out of the way, and Sarah walked into a spacious kitchen with marble countertops and stainless steel appliances. She slowly walked around the kitchen. "I would have pegged you for something more outdated, not state-of-the art, Dr. Claremont."

Dr. Claremont laughed. "You can call me Charlie, and you'd have been wrong, child. I'm not getting any younger. I'd rather have my steak in twenty minutes than forty-five. I might not be around long enough to enjoy it. You get the idea."

"Dr—" she started to say.

"Charlie," he interrupted her.

"Charlie." She smiled. "What can you tell me about the witness protection people that are hiding out in our timeline?"

"To understand that, you need to understand STEM Corporation's involvement in time travel."

"I know their involvement. I've studied their history."

He grinned and dished out a bowl of soup and slid it in front of Sarah. "You only know what they want you to know. I can guarantee you don't know the entire history. If you did, you would have shown up years before now."

"Okay. I'm ready to learn," she said, ignoring her soup while Charlie sat down. Foster filled two more bowls and then joined her at the counter.

"I'll skip the boring details, but one day, not long from now, you'll want to hear those too."

Sarah glanced at Foster, who was slurping his soup.

"Time travelers can only go into the past; never into a future that hasn't happened for them yet. There's a whole terminology on it."

"Cell memory," Sarah answered. "If I traveled I could only go back any time before my current life. I get it."

"I knew she'd be smart." Charlie smiled at Foster. "Anyway, after one of my many travels into the past…"

"To see a girl," Foster added.

"She doesn't need all that detail," Charlie said, clearing his throat. "But my Francesca, she was a beauty. Still is."

"I'm sorry, Charlie, what does this have to do with the witness protection program."

"Right," he said again as the fog cleared from his eyes. "Time travel might not been invented while I was still a child, but at my time at STEM labs, we did invented hiding witnesses in different timelines and our future ancestors must have embraced the idea."

"Francesca was the first," Foster added. "But it's not my story to tell. Sorry, Doc, continue."

"As I was saying…" Charlie cleared his throat. "We set a precedent with hiding witnesses. It was the only way to ensure their safety. What better way to get them out of harm's reach than separating the bad guys and the witnesses by putting years between them and the men that want them to disappear."

"What did they witness?" she asked.

"The best way to describe it in a way you can understand without giving you too many details is that these women were the ones responsible for putting a future Hitler-style dictator in jail for the rest of his life, and even that I'm not too sure about. They weren't inclined to tell me much."

"Okay, needing to hide makes sense," Sarah said.

"After coming back from one of my trips, I was just getting a briefing when we had incoming. Eight women and eight men, all from the same timeline in the future."

"The witnesses and their handlers?"

"Yes." Charlie's eyes glazed over as if he were remembering. "All the women looked scared. The men looked uneasy trying to understand their surroundings. It was then Mac told me they were witnesses, and I overhead the reason they'd came."

"Mac?" Sarah asked. "I don't remember a Mac in the lab's history."

"You wouldn't, you weren't working for the company yet. He was the Deputy Director of the FBI and married to Selena Bay. The CEO before her son took over."

"I knew he wasn't sitting in that spot because he's smart. They handed it to him on a silver platter," Sarah said with conviction.

"You would have liked Mac and Selena. They were very fond of your adoptive mother. They used to say that your mom might not have invented time travel, but she modernized it when she harnessed the blue electricity when creating the biofeeds," Charlie said.

"I remember the day she came home excited like she'd won the lottery."

"Your mother was a genius and STEM labs recognized her brilliance. Back to my story, the FBI Director, Mac could be an ass, but Selena had a calmness, yet had a get-shit-done vibe to her. Kind of like the one you give off."

"And they handled the witnesses?" Sarah asked, trying to get them back on track.

"They didn't. They tasked the doctor with the entire thing with only one instruction. Make them all disappear," Foster answered.

11

"And you did?" Sarah asked.

"I did everything they told me. Well, somewhat. There were a few gray areas and instructions left open to interpretation."

Sarah raised a brow.

"They told me to get rid of the files, but they weren't clear on how they wanted me to dispose of them."

Sarah's lips split into a hesitant smile. "You kept them, didn't you?"

"What makes you think that?"

"Because I would have too; otherwise, these people could get lost or forgotten in time."

"I think that was the idea," Foster added.

"That's dangerous. No one even knew they were here. What if they changed something? These women were responsible for putting a Dictator in prison in their own timeline, who's to stop them from doing something similar in ours?"

"We trusted their handlers to keep them inline." Charlie answered with a shrug of his shoulders.

"Things like that can't be undone. We wouldn't notice it, but people in the future, hell, even the scientists here, might not go back to the exact existence they left."

"More than one of them did change things." Charlie sipped at his soup. "Now eat up before your soup gets cold."

"Sir," Sarah said, "there are lives on the line. I don't mean to be rude, but I need answers, not food."

"Sarah. Food is nutrition. Nutrition gives you energy, and judging how you're dressed, you're probably dehydrated too. Eat first, and then I'll show you my prizes that you came for." Charlie leveled Sarah with his fatherly gaze.

She lifted her spoon and complied. The soup was like none she'd ever eaten. It was salty scrumptiousness. She was afraid to even ask what was in it besides the vegetables she recognized. Charlie and Foster both finished theirs. Silence ensued. All talking ceased until Sarah had sipped the last spoonful.

"Thanks, that was… different."

Charlie rinsed out his bowl and then held out his arm for Sarah to take. Foster grabbed her glass and set it on the counter before he followed behind her. He walked her into a library-office combo. Books lined the shelves, a few of the rows dusty and untouched. A desk sat against a window with the view into the pine forest. They'd positioned another table with two chairs in the middle of the room with books sitting atop and some page markers sticking out of the bindings.

"Nice office."

Charlie grinned from where he stood near one bookcase. "I'm glad you approve."

He yanked on the spine of one book, and the wall moved, giving way to another entrance. There were no windows in this one; it was all cement. Computers lined the walls with views of the building's surroundings. Another set of monitors showed what was going on at the labs as if he'd been spying, but none of that was as impressive as the computer that looked just like the quantum computer they used before new tourists arrived.

"Is this computer a replica of the one we have at the lab?" Sarah asked as she walked around it. It was like the one she used back at the compound, only this one was... different in a way she couldn't quite pinpoint. New... better parts... she couldn't quite place the difference but it was almost as if she could sense that this was the Ferrari of the computer world.

"Yes. Although this one is more advanced."

"I didn't know quantum computers could get more advanced. I thought they were know-all-be-all," Sarah said, stepping farther into the room.

"It's like any computer. With age, the specs and designs become more advanced. It still has all the knowledge as the quantum you play with, but this one has a quicker running capacity and can tell me things without an interface at the other end, like the commanders that currently give you information on the incoming time travelers."

"That's sad," Sarah said with her lips turned down.

"Sad?" Foster asked. "It's genius. He no longer has to rely on the words from someone in another time."

"It's impersonal," she countered.

"It's more honest and efficient," he argued.

"All right, children, that's enough. You're both right. Even though it is more honest, it takes the humanity out of it, and I'm not sure if that's a good thing or a bad thing," Charlie said. "But that's a debate for another day. Let's stay focused. Sarah, if you'd like to take it for a test run?"

"Don't I need access?" she asked.

"All the computers are tied together. If you've already had access, you can access this one."

Charlie gave a slight nod to Foster before he stepped out of Sarah's way, brushing her shoulder in passing and not in a screw-you kind of way, more of a I'm-still-here and I-know-I-affect-you kind of way.

She sat at one of the computers and punched a few keys, typing in the term "witness protection" into the search bar. Faces lit the screen. Some she instantly recognized, and others she'd never seen before.

"Is that…" Sarah said, stepping closer.

"Professor Abigale Stillman. I believe she's working in aeronautics at the labs now and is married to Dr. Stillman."

"She is." Sarah's mouth parted.

"She was witness protection number 3," Charlie said and pointed to the man with her. "And I believe you know her handler."

She recognized him immediately. It was a younger picture of Dr. Stillman who worked in the infirmary. How could Sarah not have known that people she worked with weren't from her time?

"Don't be surprised," Charlie said with a sigh. "They were brilliant in the future. It makes sense the lab would keep them on the payroll. How do you think the lab has been making their breakthroughs?"

"By breaking the very laws they're forcing the visiting time travelers to adhere to," Sarah whispered crossing her arms over her chest. "Who gets to decide which laws are okay to break?"

"Yes, well, there are exceptions to every rule and they do have the future Time Magistrate who governs the travelers."

"Did they know about these witnesses?"

Charlie shrugged. "Let's just say, they had all the right paperwork, now if some of it was forged, I couldn't tell you."

"The Stillman's have children," Sarah said, crossing her arms over her chest. That was one of the biggest rules that they had to adhere to. Absolutely no pregnancies with a time traveler or someone from a different timeline.

"That's a gray area since they're both time travelers that came from the same timeline. They sanctioned it."

Sarah scrolled down the wall of faces, stopping at the one she was most worried about. "What can you tell me about Emma?"

She clicked the file label next to Emma's name and pulled up a complete dossier with aliases, jobs, and background, including passport information. Next to her files were those of her handler. A man that she'd never seen before. His name was John Smith.

"John Smith, really?" Sarah asked, glancing back at Charlie. "Couldn't you guys think of anything more original back then?"

"That wasn't the point," Charlie said. "They weren't here to be original. They were here to blend in."

"That will make him difficult to find."

"John has called the Glades Cemetery his home for two years." Foster reached over her shoulder and clicked a few buttons, and a graveyard appeared on the screen. "He died from a gunshot wound during a home invasion robbery."

12

Sarah rested her hand on her neck. The thought of Emma being alone in this time with no one to watch over her or help her ripped at Sarah's heart. Everyone deserved some type of family, even if John was just her guardian and hired gun.

"I assume the handlers and the witnesses lived together?"

"Yes." He answered.

"Okay, so where was Emma when her handler was killed?" Sarah asked.

"No one has had eyes on her since she showed up with you."

Foster spun around the chair and rested his hand on the desk, leaning over into her face. "What emotional state was she in when you got her?"

"I guess you could say traumatized. Her clothes were covered in blood. She and one of our tourists were fleeing from gunshots. She made it through the portal, and he didn't."

"Tourist?" Charlie asked.

"That's what I call the time traveler scientists. Logan Cartwright just came into 2018 about six months ago. He was supposed to be doing aquatic research out in the ocean. I can't even imagine how their paths crossed."

Charlie spun Sarah's chair around to face the computer. "Run facial recognition for any signs of Emma."

"Your computer can do that? Wouldn't it be too much to process?"

"It will take some time, but this computer is capable of so much more," Charlie said. "You'll want to pull up Logan's information too."

"Okay," Sarah said as her fingers flew across the holographic screen in front of the quantum computer. She rested her hand on the reader, and when the screen came to life, she typed in Logan's name.

Sarah's mouth parted as she stared at the information that came up. Logan's picture popped up with his statistics. A message flashed the words, Time Recalculating.

"What does that mean?"

"That, my dear, means that Logan is still alive and his outcome is pending," Charlie said.

"Will this machine tell you where to find him?"

"It only tells us at the moment or ancient history

for your time travelers. It can't predict a future that hasn't happened. This moment for Logan has never happened before. It's new."

"So that's a big no," Foster added.

"Fine. We'll do this investigation the old-fashioned way."

Sarah pulled out her phone and took pictures of the witness protection time travelers. There was no way she'd take the original file and let something happen to it.

"Take Foster with you. He's memorized the files."

Heat climbed in Sarah's cheeks. "That's unnecessary. My people will help get this sorted."

"Sarah." Charlie rested his palms on her arms and stared into her eyes. "Did you ever stop to think that one of your people from the agency might be involved? Or, at the very least, be responsible for the leak? What do you think Logan was running from in the first place?"

"To help Emma," she answered.

"Whose only reason for being in 2018 is because she's in the witness protection program."

"That information was classified even from my eyes, and besides, who in this time would want her dead? One of the other seven in the program? No one, because they're hiding out too. So who else could it be? My theory is Emma, or maybe both she and Logan, got into something over their heads and the bad guys chasing them want something entirely unrelated to time travel."

"And the incident for the lab blowing up was just a coincidence?" Foster asked, crossing his arms over his chest and staring down at her. "I don't believe in coincidences."

He had a point, not that she'd tell him. She didn't believe in coincidences either. The agency and Emma were both targets, but the questions remaining were, who was pulling the triggers and why?

Foster grabbed a charged biofeed cache and strapped it to his arm before stuffing things into his backpack.

"He's not going," she argued.

"You need him," Charlie said.

"He'll be in my way."

Foster was checking his weapons for bullets before he stuffed those and more gadgets into the backpack.

He glanced up to find them both staring at him. She narrowed her eyes.

"You weren't listening, were you?" Charlie asked.

"No," he answered, sliding the backpack up his arm. He punched GPS coordinates into his biofeed.

"You aren't going," she growled.

"You can't stop me, princess," Foster answered. "Charlie bringing you in was a courtesy. I'm not one of your time travelers you can boss around."

The portal opened behind him, directly into a familiar-looking warehouse where Logan had been running and was being shot at.

Foster shrugged and stepped through the portal into the warehouse and glanced back at her. "Well, are you coming?"

It was seconds away from closing when she jumped through and fell into his arms.

13

Sarah pushed out of Foster's arms, ignoring the heat claiming her cheeks. He unzipped his back-pack and pulling out a stun gun and a 9 mm. He handed her the stun gun. "Try not to shoot me."

"I can't make any promises," she said.

Walking behind him through the warehouse, looking for the same point of view she'd witnessed when Logan had been running to the time slip he'd sent Emma through. The large space was filled with abandoned shelves and old machinery covered in thick dust. The sounds of their footsteps echoed in the large space. Vagrants or teens with too much time had spray painted graffiti on some outer walls.

She slowed, looking over her shoulder until she spotted the angle from where the time slip had opened. Sarah ran her finger over the electrical smudge left on the metal shelves. "The time slip opened here."

She kept her head down and searched the floor until she found the semi-dried smudge on the floor. Goosebumps covered her arms, and she swallowed hard, squatting next to the blood.

"Logan went down here," she announced, taking in the surroundings.

"That should make this easier." Foster rested his hand on her arm and lifted her out of the way. Taking several steps backward, he pulled two pairs of glasses out of the backpack and handed her one. "Let's take a look."

She slowly slid them up her nose and glanced around the warehouse. The dark tint on the glass had her lowering them from her eyes. The darkness made her feel vulnerable and blind.

Foster grinned and slid her glasses back into place. He pressed something on the glasses, making his face come into view as if lifting a curtain. "Give me a minute to sync it to the time we need."

Sarah glanced around the room. Images and people crowded in around her as the surrounding walls changed from pure land to a house and eventually to the warehouse they were standing in. The structures and associated people from different times appeared to fade in and out. Everything was muted as if she was standing in the center of a moving picture and the set was in constant transition around her until it slowed. Phantom images of people moved around and through her as if she were a ghost. It was as if this location had its own life and she was witnessing everything that happened over several centuries. It was a rush of energy she'd never felt. Excitement skirted her spine. She wanted to take it all in, and look at everything but there was too much to see. She turned in place unable to speak.

The surrounding people slowed until the building became like where they currently stood. The lighting coming through one window had shifted on the ground, different from what they were looking at.

"Here we go," Foster said, taking her by the arm and pulling her back against his chest. "This is all holographic from the residual energy of that time and space."

Sarah's heart quickened as Logan and Emma came running around the empty shelves headed in her direction. Blood oozed down a cut on Logan's forehead as he hurried to punch his biofeed.

The sound was completed muted. "Why can't I hear him?"

"These glasses only help you see the energy. Charlie hasn't developed anything that can help us hear the sounds from those times."

Logan and Emma crouched around a dusty shelf while Logan punched in GPS coordinates into his biofeed. He tore a piece of paper in two and handed her the top half. He closed her hand around the paper tight before nodding once more. They both peered behind them and ran for the wall where the time slip was opening.

It was weird being able to see herself in the other room. The way it looked from this angle watching herself and Jonathan in Crenshaw's motel room. It seemed like it had all just happened.

Sarah took a step toward Logan's fallen body. It was hard to watch this as a witness and not interfere. She glanced toward Crenshaw's room again to find herself and Jonathan shooting at the men coming up behind Logan. The bullet she'd shot whizzed through her like she wasn't in the way, landing in a wooden beam past where she stood.

Jonathan's bullet didn't miss. The gunman fell to the ground.

The time slip closed, thrusting the warehouse back into darkness. Logan was using all of his effort to pull himself into safety behind one rack. Logan slid his half of the torn paper beneath one riser seconds before gunmen came into view. Each had their weapons pointed at his head.

The muscles bulging from beneath their military fatigues and dark clothes made them look lethal even without the night vision gadgets and ammo belts wrapped around their waists. These men meant business.

"This is worse than I thought," Foster whispered.

Logan dropped his weapon and held up his hands.

Two of the gunmen lifted him under the arms and dragged Logan's body down the hall. They dropped him at the booted feet of another man.

Sarah's hand flew to cover her mouth. She'd do anything to go back and do it different. She would launch head-first into the fight to protect Logan. She should have crossed that threshold and fought with everything she had to help get Logan to safety. This man oozed power, and there was no question he was the leader in this deadly game of cat and mouse.

His white hair stood up in a high and tight cut. Deep-rooted lines around his face held tinges of pink scars from previous battles. *Typical GI Joe.*

"Do you know them?" Sarah asked as she followed behind them. The hair on her neck stood on end as she struggled to watch, hoping for the best but mentally preparing for the worst.

"Yeah, I know him. Adam Kemper is a time enforcement commander," Foster said, walking around the man. The enforcer had a scar line that ran down by his cheek. Tattoos poked out beneath his sleeves.

"I've never heard of a time enforcement commander. Is there some time travel law enforcement community I haven't been privy to?"

"Yes and no," he said, tilting his head while staring at the guy.

"And… are you going to explain?"

"No."

Okay, then she'd do her own digging later. She moved closer to Kemper and watched his lips, trying to read what he was saying. "How do you know Kemper?"

"I used to be part of his team."

14

All questions swirling in and out of Sarah's mind vanished as the Ice Man, Commander Kemper, slapped something onto Logan's wrist and pressed a button. The cuffs looked like the ones Sarah liked to use. Only these had a few more buttons and were black instead of silver.

Kemper pressed a button, and a time slip opened. Unlike where Sarah sent Crenshaw into a holding cell with bars, this place had vibrant blue energy streams like the ones produced in the transponder room when tourists arrived. Only these energy streams formed a similar containment area.

The energetic vibration sucked Logan out of the warehouse and into the holding cell.

"Tell me you know where that room is." Sarah yanked the glasses off her face as the aggravation and anger seeped through her core. She stomped over to where Logan had stashed the other portion of the paper and pulled it out. She unfolded it. Drops of Logan's blood were smeared in the corner.

"I know it," Foster answered, his voice full of resignation.

Sarah's heart clenched tight. The paper that Logan had hidden contained a list of numbers. She took a picture with her cell before handing it to Foster. "Does this mean anything to you?"

He stared at the paper, and the corners of his mouth slid into a frown. "How in the hell...."

"I'll take that as a yes," Sarah answered.

"We can't stay here." Foster punched a few buttons into his biofeed before grabbing her hand and pulling her through.

The familiar smell of forest surrounded her. The cabin where she'd first met Foster sat just through the trees.

"What were those numbers?" she asked, tilting her head and watching the hesitation play across his face.

"I....just can't tell you." A shadow passed by the window, blocking the light inside. "And you can't tell anyone about me, the doctor, or what you saw. This is so much bigger than just Emma and the other witnesses."

"You said you worked with Kemper," Sarah said, taking a step back. "That means you aren't from my time either."

Foster dropped his gaze. "No."

"How did you get here? I haven't seen a report on you or Kemper, and our machine is the only vehicle for time travel."

"Our aim was to arrive unnoticed," Foster said.

"That doesn't answer my question. Who sent you, and how in the hell did you get here?"

"I'm afraid I can't tell you that. It could change things and do more damage. Sarah, trust me. I know it's not in your nature, but just this once, trust a stranger to have your best interest."

"I don't know you." She shook her head. The only thing that mattered was getting Emma and Logan back alive, fixing the destruction at the compound, and finding the witnesses to protect them. Accomplishing those things would uncomplicate Sarah's life. "Where is the holding cell, and what do those numbers mean?"

"I can't tell you. Not yet. I can't risk you'll go storm the place to get him out. We need to do this right before more people get hurt."

"Foster—"

"I'll meet you back here in twenty-four hours with an update on Logan. Go back to the compound and pretend like everything is fine. Your life and those of your coworkers depend on it."

"I'm not leaving here until you give me some answers."

The door to the cabin squeaked open. Sarah spun in that direction.

"Sarah," Jonathan whispered. "What are you doing out there?"

Sarah glanced back to find Foster gone. She stepped out of the tree line. "How did you know I was here?"

"Dr. Bay told me you were tracking down a lead and had to use the safe house," he said, holding the door open for her.

Sarah was punching the coordinates into her biofeed when Jonathan covered her fingers with his hand.

"Sarah, something's isn't adding up." Jonathan's brows dipped. "In addition to Emma, several employees are missing. We've checked the compound, the hospitals, and even tried to track them via GPS."

"Any hits on their locations?"

"None. Every single person we're looking for went offline. What's even stranger is that Dr. Bay has brought in some new people to help track them."

"White hair, military cut?"

"How did you know?" Jonathan asked.

"Crap. We have to find them first."

"I need to take you back to Dr. Bay."

"I can't go back, not until I know what the hell is going on," Sarah growled.

"Go back and report in. If you don't, he'll send

someone else to look for you. They traced the point of impact to the infirmary, specifically to Logan's biofeed. Someone rigged it to explode, and you brought it into the compound. They have questions."

All hope vanished, deflating Sarah's shoulders. Had she been played? Logan had been punching something into his biofeed while he'd been hiding with Emma only seconds before he sent Emma through the time slip. Was that the whole point of sending her back? Those thoughts swirled in Sarah's head as she finished punching the coordinates into her biofeed and stepped through the portal when it opened. Jonathan followed her in.

Dr. Bay was still in Area 2 and surrounded by the men that Sarah had seen inside the warehouse. The killers, the chasers, the men who had Logan.

Sarah made a beeline in Dr. Bay's direction, ignoring the stares of the other lab employees around her. Only a handful of those stares were accusing looks; the rest were in the form of pity. Both aggravated the piss out of her.

Two men with guns flanked Adam Kemper as he talked to Dr. Bay. One might think she'd be have been told about a futuristic time police-warden hanging out in 2018. Obviously, she'd been left out of that loop. How many others had there been?

Knowing about the police warden was one thing. Keeping her mouth shut and pretending to be clueless was something she wasn't sure she could pull off.

15

"Sarah, this is Adam Kemper. He's from Internal Affairs and has questions to ask you about Emma and Logan."

Funny. What did he think she could tell him he didn't already know? Or maybe this was a fishing expedition to see how much she knew.

Foster's words of warning, his urgency and pleas to trust him flitted through her mind. There was no one she trusted. How could she? Even her coworkers were keeping secrets. And she considered those people her friends. Fear yawning in her gut overrode the feelings of emptiness. She'd been alone before. She liked it better that way, but this…this was taking it to a whole new level.

"Sir," Sarah said, clasping her hands together.

Adam Kemper's gaze slid down Sarah's yoga

pants and back up to her jacket. "Sarah, do you have any idea where Emma is?"

She stared into his eyes, determined to look unwavering. "No."

"Do you know why she and Logan planned to blow up the facility?"

Sarah's lips twitched. "You have no proof they planned this. If this is a witch hunt, you're in the wrong year."

Kemper's jaw ticked. "You brought her in, Agent Weston. We could hold you responsible for the damage to the facility."

Sarah stepped closer, into Kemper's face. "One might lay blame on the men shooting at Logan. That was the reason they searched for me. The fact that Emma could move between time slips without dying told me enough. She not only knew about our facility but how it works, considering she had to have drunk the blue liquid stabilizing agent to cross the threshold. If I were you, Kemper, I'd take a close look at who knew her secret before laying blame where evidence is lacking."

"Sarah. That's enough," Dr. Bay growled in warning. "Why don't you update us on what you found when you went looking for Dr. Charlie Claremont."

"He wasn't any help, just like you said. He was grumpy and wanted nothing to do with me."

"Anyone with him?" Kemper asked.

"She returned alone," Jonathan said. "If that's all,

gentlemen, Sarah and I still have a ton of work to do and situations to contain."

She'd turned to leave when Kemper rested his hand on her arm. "Agent Weston, we aren't done yet."

Sarah's gaze landed on Kemper's hand, and she raised her brow. "Unless you plan to arrest me, I suggest you remove your hand."

He made no move to release her, so she knocked it off herself.

"Kemper, wasn't it? Exactly what time frame are you from because, in this time, when a man lays his hand on a woman's arm, it better be welcome or you might lose it." Sarah narrowed her eyes, ignoring the need to poke his chest to prove her point. "They didn't hire me for my analytical skills. They hired me to keep the tourists in line. What exactly is your job?"

The men behind Kemper had been watching their surroundings and turned their gazes to Sarah. Even they could feel the threat she was issuing.

Kemper's heated gaze held hers before ice covered his stony features. "You're free to go... for now."

Sarah turned without saying another word and continued walking toward Diana, who was watching from a doorway. She was holding a file close to her chest. Her worried gaze never strayed from Sarah's.

Jonathan followed her, ushering them all into the makeshift office and closing the door.

"You know how to make friends," Diana teased.

"What do you know about him?" Sarah asked, standing at the blinds staring out at the white-haired commander who was barking orders to his men.

"Not much, I'm afraid. Someone issued him top-level clearance a month ago. He reports only to Dr. Bay and Eleonore, and I don't think they call his shots," Diana said, putting her phone on speaker.

"All hell breaks loose when you visit me in the basement. I'm going to restrict your access if it happens again." Ritter's voice was a nice surprise.

"Where are you?" Sarah asked.

"In the basement. The fire didn't touch my area. It only disabled some access lines, but I've already rewired everything. I'm up and running, and you'll be glad I am because, after you left, I started digging."

Sarah exchanged a confused look with Diana and Jonathan. "What exactly were you digging for?"

"You mentioned that Emma was with Logan, and for the life of me, I couldn't figure out how Logan and the woman met, so I backtracked Logan's GPS coordinates looking for any anomalies."

"And you found one?" Sarah asked.

"I found more than one, Sarah. I found ten in the last month, and considering how Diana's down to working with an abacus, I pulled the surveillance for her."

"Aw, thanks, Ritter. You know, you and I should totally work more together," Diana cooed.

"Can we keep this on point?" Jonathan sighed in aggravation.

"Right," Ritter said. "Show them what I found."

Diana slipped out the picture of Logan, Emma, and both Doctor Stillman and his wife. They were sitting in the back of a coffee shop. The angle was from across the street.

"Where was the camera?"

"The new bank across the street. It wasn't scheduled to open until a week later, but they were in testing mode and lucky for us had it turned on."

"I'll check out the Stillman residence for any clues," Jonathan said as the portal opened around him and he stepped through.

"If Doc Stillman could lie about not knowing Emma, what else is he lying about?"

"I'll cross reference Stillman's GPS coordinates with Logan's, looking for same place, same time incidents in the last month."

"Make it a year and call me back with the findings, not Dr. Bay, until we know what the hell is going on," Sarah said.

"You got it," he answered, and Diana disconnected the call.

"What aren't you telling me?" Diana asked as Sarah took the picture from her hand and punched in numbers on her biofeed to take her back to the beach house.

"Sarah, you need to deal with Ziggy Carmichael.

You can't put him off any longer, especially now that I've limited resources to stop him from exposing us."

"Let me change and deal with this picture, and he'll be my next stop. I promise." Not that Sarah had any idea what she'd be doing when she got there. Diana didn't need to know that. Right now, Sarah would settle for a house fire just to buy her some more time to deal with the more pressing matters.

16

Sarah watched the flames dance in the air as she moved them back and forth across the picture of Doctor Stillman, Logan, and Emma. Keeping it would only prompt more questions than she had answers for. She knew Emma was a witness, along with Dr. Stillman's wife, and that Stillman himself was an asset of the program they'd spent years trying to keep under wraps. She still didn't know the exact reason they'd been placed into witness protection. Their involvement with Emma made sense even if Logan's didn't.

Logan's face withered into black soot as the flame crawled across the glossy photo.

She tossed the remains in the fireplace and took a long overdue shower and changed her clothes. She replaced her yoga pants with jeans and forewent the white suits she liked to wear.

She sat down on the bed to put on her shoes. The

weight of the day's activities rested heavy on her shoulders. Any other time, she would take a few minutes and relax to catch her breath, but not tonight. Tonight's work could mean the difference between life and death.

Sarah clamped on her biofeed and pressed the GPS coordinates for the alley behind Ziggy's apartment. The running joke at the agency was whoever dealt with Ziggy had to bring back hot, fresh donuts from the nearby bakery across the street.

Sarah stepped out of the slip and closed it. The rundown building had seen better days. It wasn't in the worst neighborhood, but it wasn't in the best either.

The smell of baked bread drifted from the bakery across the street, and the scent reminded her that she hadn't eaten anything but soup in hours. Eating would have to wait until she dealt with Ziggy.

She entered the apartment building and proceeded down the hall. Ziggy lived on the bottom floor near a back exit. It had come in handy on more than one trip to check in on what the hacker had been up to.

She knocked on the door and listened for any sound coming from the other side.

A man in his thirties walked out from a door across the hall. Tall, Dark, and Sexy winked as he passed her, continuing down the hall toward the front exit of the building. Content she was alone, she punched in the numbers for inside Ziggy's home and stepped through the slip they'd placed in the door. It was as if Ziggy himself had opened the door and invited her inside.

The living room was dark and quiet other than the hum from the fridge and a ticking clock hanging on the wall. The scent of donuts hit her in the face. She inhaled a deep breath and released it, trying to stifle the growl of her stomach. Fantasy posters and memorabilia lined the walls, and miniature collectibles overflowed the bookshelf.

She eased down the hall and pressed her ear to the bedroom door to listen for anything other than the humming and whine of a computer.

Nothing.

She slowly turned the knob and eased the door open to find the room empty. She stepped inside and sat down at the desk, bringing the computer to life. She inserted the thumb drive containing the virus into his computer to uploading the hidden files for an easy off-site execution. The virus would kill anything and everything she deemed classified with a single stroke of the keyboard from miles away. They should have thought of planting a dormant virus years ago. It would have saved them the trouble from countless returns to the repeat offender.

"I knew it." Ziggy's voice had her spinning around. "Which agency are you with? CIA, Homeland, MIB?"

Sarah pulled out her badge and flipped it open to

show to the tall lanky computer geek. Ziggy was wearing a white shirt with mustard stains beneath his plaid shirt. Unruly curls stuck out from beneath the beanie on his head. "FBI."

"Uh-huh, FBI doesn't employ supermodels. They employ women that look like dudes," Ziggy said, walking farther into the room. He closed the door behind him and flicked the lock.

Supermodel? Points for kid, although that wouldn't make her forget why she was here.

"I know my rights. You can't be in here without a warrant," he stated.

"I didn't need one. I thought I heard someone screaming help from inside your home." Sarah slid to block his view of the computer so he couldn't see the damage she was doing.

"You're lying. Get out."

Sarah shrugged. "I should arrest you."

Not that she would have. She'd never arrested anyone before in her life. Well, she sent time travelers to the holding cell for transport home but never an innocent who was just trying to prove time travel was real.

"On what grounds?"

"Deceiving the public with crap you know isn't real," Sarah said and flicked the bouncy head of the alien on the desk.

"I've met a real time traveler, and I can prove it,

not that it's any of your business. Just who the hell you are."

"My name isn't important, but obstructing justice is." Sarah raised her brow and crossed her arms over her chest.

"What justice am I obstructing?"

"Marvin Crenshaw escaped a psychiatric ward, and you were the last person he was in contact with. So tell me how can you prove it?"

He held up a video camera and pressed play. The screen showed Sarah stepping out of a time slip. "I caught not only him but you, and you two aren't the only ones." Ziggy stepped over to the computer and yanked out the thumb drive and tossed it at her.

"Did you honestly think that I'd put my prize intelligence on my home computer knowing you guys have hacked me and erased files in the past?" He turned his smug smile at her and slapped the video feed closed. "When my radar started going wonky the last three weeks, I recorded stuff."

"What radar?" Sarah asked, dropping her folded arms to her side.

"Oh no, you don't. If I tell you, then my radar will be next item to mysteriously disappear."

"Okay so don't tell me. I'll take you in, and you can explain it to the judge, where it will be public knowledge so everyone knows about your radar."

"I knew Marvin. He provided me with a package and a download. The package contained pictures of people that have been here in our time for the last three centuries."

Sarah's heart raced. Maybe Ziggy knew more than they thought.

"Mostly women. They live among us. They work among us."

"Who?" she asked, curious where he was going with this.

"The aliens."

17

A liens. Right. No one would question if Ziggy ended up in a loony bin one day. He was the quintessential conspiracy nut. The life-sized cut-out of Sasquatches wearing tinfoil hats would be enough to convince most he was crazy, but crazy or not, he had a video of Sarah appearing out of thin air, and he claimed to have more.

"Who else is on your video?" Sarah asked.

"I'm not telling you." He slid the phone back in his pocket. "You'll make all my footage disappear."

"You've got an active imagination. What are you, twelve?" she asked with her finger on a comic book that she slid out of her way.

"For years, the government has been covering up time travel and aliens, and I'm going to prove it."

Sarah rested her fist on her hips. "What makes

you think the government even knows what's going on and we aren't just some secret organization?"

His eyes momentarily widened before he tsked and shook his head. He pulled out his phone and showed Sarah another video. "Normal people don't dress like GI Joe."

He held the video up for Sarah to see. The trigger-happy Ice Man from the compound stepped out of a time slip wearing standard military fatigues. Seeing Kemper didn't surprise her. It was the person standing with him. Jonathan.

Anger surged through her body as she squeezed her fist, digging her fingernails into the palm of her hands. Her heart crumbled into a million pieces. Jonathan knew these people, and he hadn't told her.

"Where and when was that taken?"

"Two weeks ago," he said, sliding the phone back into his pocket.

"Where?" she asked.

He shook his head and pressed his lips together.

"Where!" Sarah demanded, grabbing him by his graphic T-shirt.

"Nope," he said.

Sarah shoved him out of her hold and punched numbers into her biofeed. Electricity sizzled around them until a circle formed and a time slip opened. A pine scent drifted to her nose. The safe house was located in the distance on the other side of the slip.

"Cool." Ziggy was about to put his hand through the opening when she yanked it back.

"Not cool. There is a special serum you need to drink to go through one. Without the serum, you'll disintegrate. Those men that you recorded kidnapped my friend, and if you don't tell me where in the hell that video was taken, your next and last trip will be adding ashes to the forest floor."

"You're threatening me?"

"Damn right I am." She grabbed him again and leaned him near the opening, ignoring all rationale that tried to calm her mind. This wasn't her. Twenty-four hours ago, she would have never opened a time slip in front of someone who didn't know the secret, much less threaten to push him through if he didn't tell her what she wanted to know. Maybe she was the one who needed the loony bin or at least a vacation when this was all over. Her nice and neat compact world was crumbling before her eyes and taking part of her with it. "This is your last chance, Ziggy. Where in the hell was that video taken?"

He swallowed hard. "You will kill me anyway now that I know your secret."

"Fuck." She growled and pulled him away from the opening just as it closed. "I want to save my friend. Why are you making this so difficult?" she yelled and swiped at the figurines on the desk, sending them flying across the room.

"The liquid is blue, isn't it?" Ziggy asked, unzipping his backpack.

Sarah pulled her gun and pointed it at Ziggy as he turned around with a vial of the blue liquid in his hand. "Where did you get that?"

"Marvin," Ziggy answered. "I'll make you a deal. If I drink this and tell you where that video was taken, you promise to take me through a portal?"

It was official; Sarah would be fired for divulging company secrets. Not only would she be fired but her name would also be smeared through the mud and all because Ziggy Carmichael had information she needed.

"I'll do you one better," Sarah said, "Give me all of your evidence, tell me where the video was shot, and not only will I take you through a portal, but if you can prove to me that you can keep your mouth shut, I'll get you a job working with us."

An alarm sounded in the room that had Sarah turning in place. Ziggy had his phone out again, checking the screen.

"They're here." Panic laced his words. "What are we going to do?"

"Who's' here?" She asked.

He turned the phone for her to see that Kemper was in the alley with his gun toting goons.

Sarah shrugged. "We haven't made a deal. I'll just leave you here to work things out with them."

Ziggy grabbed her arm as she punched in numbers

on her biofeed. Ziggy uncapped the blue liquid and guzzled it. "Take me."

"Where's the evidence?"

He grabbed his backpack and held it up.

"Is that everything?" she asked as pounding sounded on the apartment door.

Ziggy reached beneath his mattress and grabbed a mail package. Clutching both to his chest, he squealed as his front door burst open.

"It's everything. Let's go."

Sarah opened the portal and stepped through. Ziggy closed his eyes as he stepped over the threshold.

"Breathe," she whispered, and Ziggy opened his eyes.

His bedroom door burst open, and Ice Man was grabbing his gun. Sarah pulled Ziggy behind her and punched in the numbers on her biofeed. The portal closed as a bullet zipped through.

Sarah was already opening another portal, pulling Ziggy through the bowels of Little China and keeping him moving through the streets as she opened the access to other places, dragging him through ten different locations in an attempt to lose Kemper and his goons from her trail.

Every time they stepped into a new destination, he wanted to explore and watched like a kid at an amusement park seeing the rides for the first time.

"Tracking me should keep them busy for at least

an hour. Maybe longer," Sarah added, pulling out her phone and dialing Diana's number. "If anyone, including Jonathan, asks for my GPS, give them somewhere else and trust no one."

"Who are you talking to?" Ziggy asked.

"Who's with you, and what's going on?" Diana asked.

"Ziggy Carmichael."

"Sweet, I'm famous with you people."

"Shut up," she growled.

"Who me?" Diana asked.

"No, not you, Diana. I was talking to Ziggy. Listen, Adam Kemper and his band of trigger-happy guys showed up at Ziggy's. Did you tell him where I was going?"

"I didn't tell him, but I told Jonathan."

Just freakin perfect. "Listen, I don't have time to explain. Just promise me that you won't give them my GPS or where I've been for the last two hours. Shoot your computer if you have to so they can't follow me."

"Sarah." Warning sounded in Diana's voice. "Jonathan is one of us. He'd never betray you."

Minutes ago she'd thought the same thing. "I need to be off the grid."

"So lose your bracelet thingy," Ziggy said.

"This bracelet thingy is like your back door escape out of the building. Without it, we can be cornered and captured."

"Can't you just call the police on those guys and have them picked up?" he asked.

"He has a point," Diana said through the speaker. "I can always leak some information to slow them down while sending them on a wild goose chase. I heard Antarctica was pretty this time of year. Can you imagine trying to conjure power where there isn't any?"

"I need to find some place for Ziggy to lie low until we get this situated."

"You're going to trust leaving him alone?" Diana's voice deepened in disapproval. "Just put him in a holding cell."

"Hey," Ziggy argued. "I'm not going to tell on my future boss."

"Sarah, you didn't…." Diana growled.

"He has information I need. It was either that or kill him. Let Human Resources know that I picked Natalie's replacement."

"Who is Natalie, and why did you need to replace her?" Ziggy asked.

"My last assistant. She got lost somewhere in time." Sarah held up her biofeed to show him. "Biofeeds and time jumping aren't toys. We lost her signal a long time ago."

Ziggy's mouth parted. "And you can't find her?"

Sarah shook her head. "Nope. We sent out a search and rescue time travel group to her last known location, and there was no sign of her."

18

Sarah opened one more portal and gestured for Ziggy to enter.

"Why are we leaving again? There's a perfectly fine hotel near here," Ziggy said.

"Because until that phone call my steps were traceable."

"I know where we can go where no one will look," Ziggy offered.

Sarah debated the pros and cons of where she could take Ziggy to keep him safe. Her colleagues knew every move she'd make. Not that she could trust all of them. They told her all the time she was predictable. But Ziggy... they had no idea where he might go or what he might do if he were hiding from people like her. "Where? And don't tell me it's your mother's basement."

A smile lit his face. "It's not my mother's basement, but you will not like it."

Why would that be any different from anything right now? "Where?"

"The UG," he said enthusiastically, as if she should have understood what that meant.

"What the hell is the UG? Is it a strip joint or something?"

"It's the Underground, a whole community of people like me."

"Conspiracy nuts?"

"No." He looked insulted. "More like hackers who spend their time trying to prove the government is hiding things from us," he said as he walked away.

"For the love of all that's holy…" She grabbed his arm. "You want me to take you to a place filled with hackers like you? Have you lost your mind?" She squeezed her forehead. "I feel a headache forming."

"No one will ever look for you there. I'll just introduce you as my girlfriend."

"No," Sarah answered without hesitation.

"Sister," he offered.

"No."

"Well, it has to be someone I trust, or they'll never accept you in. Trust me when I tell you that you don't want these guys poking into your cyber footprint."

"Fine. I'm your cousin from Florida," she said, glancing up and down the sidewalk. "But first I need the location of that video and the proof you were sent."

She took him by the arm and steered him across the street to a strip club. She paid for their cover and stepped inside.

The half-naked woman dancing on the stage entertained Ziggy while Sarah went through Ziggy's backpack and opened the package that Marvin Crenshaw had sent him.

She pulled out the biofeed and set it on the table. Next, a map with the STEM facility location circled and a magnetic card. The design was holographic and looked unlike anything used in this time. She flipped through the pictures of all the analysts that had been sent to Ziggy's room using a time a slip. He had a boatload of proof spanning the last year. This wasn't something random. This was methodical and calculating.

Unbelievable. He really knew all this time. She lifted her gaze to find him watching her. "Why didn't you put any of this on the internet?"

"I didn't have enough information, and besides, if I did, then you might have stopped coming around."

He moved some pictures out of the way to show a few of her team going into the bakery. "If Mrs. Kalinski knew she was serving time travelers…" Ziggy snorted.

"We aren't the time travelers, and neither are

these people you've got pictures of. They work with me, but they don't travel through anything more than time slips like you just did. Cleaning up after the others isn't a glamorous job, but it's needed work to keep the balance."

"I guess that makes you lonely. It's okay. I don't have any friends either. They're all screen names. I looked one of them up once, and she was a bored mother of three teens. She was old enough to be my mom."

Sarah shoved the information back inside, along with Marvin's biofeed. "Okay, so where was that picture taken, and how did you know to be in that location at that exact time?"

"I got a tip. It came in the form of an email. I tried to trace it to see if it was legit but the IP address was pinging around the world and never stopped. Whoever sent it was good, better than most if you know what I mean."

"So you went there by yourself? Were you worried you were walking into a trap?" Sarah tilted her head.

"That's why it's such a weird angle. I hid the cameras up in the tree."

"And where is this place?"

"Underneath a bridge in Central Park."

Sarah rose from her spot. "We're going to go to the Underground, and you're going to draw me a map to that bridge."

"Okay, but you're wasting your time. They've only used that bridge twice, and that was weeks ago."

He rose from his seat to follow her out the door. "I followed them once."

She slowed and turned to face him. "That was dangerous."

"I can show you where they went."

"Why don't you just tell me where they went?" She grabbed his arm and walked.

He lifted his thumb and leaned in. "The UG entrance is back that way."

She spun him around and shifted his backpack up her arm. "Where did they go when you followed?"

"They went onto a freighter at the port. I tried to follow, but I didn't have a badge to get on the property, and it had armed guards."

Sarah and Ziggy walked for a mile in silence down alleyways in a maze. There came the point when she wondered if he were going in alternate routes on purpose in hopes she wouldn't be able to find it again. With the right GPS coordinates, she could go straight there without being invited.

He stopped her and jostled a trashcan out of the way. Behind it was a hole in the wall that led to steps below the building. Another door later and they were in the old subway tunnels. These passageways might be unused, but they were well kept. There was no dust, no rats, and no trash. The corridors were clean and brightly lit.

"Who's paying for the power?" she asked.

"All you need to know is we aren't taking it from residents, just bad guys who thought they had good online hiding places." He grinned.

He pulled her to a stop outside an entrance into what looked like an old substation. He looked her over and pulled down her sleeve to cover her biofeed. Taking off his extra plaid shirt, he tied it around her waist before removing his beanie and pulling it down over her head. "You still look like a cover model, but this is better. You look like a nerd cover model. Here goes nothing. Just stick close to me and act like you've done this before."

She followed him into the darkened area filled with computer desks and large screens hanging on the walls. Someone was playing a video game on one. On another was something much different. It looked like how she'd imagined the internal workings of the internet might look, a string of letters and numbers running down the screen.

"Ziggy, my man, who is this fine specimen you brought into our crib?"

"I'm Sarah, his cousin from Florida." Sarah held out her hand to shake his.

He looked at it as if it were a foreign object before turning his gaze back to Ziggy and raising his brow.

Ziggy lowered her hand. "Forgive her, Zeke. That's how they greet all the snowbirds in Florida."

"What's your poison, princess?" Zeke asked, gesturing to the entire room. "We have gaming for our downtime. We have a hacking job in the works, and we have the Kill Joy club."

"Kill Joy?" she asked.

"Kill Joy is our own personal sugar daddy. We look for the most perverted, sadistic asshats on the web, and we confiscate their porn and dirty deeds. With a little persuasion not to go to the police, they pay our light bill. It's the way we make a living so to speak."

"By blackmailing scum." Sarah's smile slipped.

"Aunt Betty never thought I was an angel," Ziggy said, keeping the cover.

"It's not like that, Goldilocks," Zeke said. "We're the anonymous tips that send the terrible ones to the cops, and we give half the money to the victims with the promise the scumbags will leave them alone."

"Blackmailers with heart. That's an interesting concept."

"Yo, Zigman, I don't think your cousin approves."

"Oh, it's not that, Zeke. She's just had a long trip in and isn't use to our culture."

Sarah held up her hands. "No judgment here. I appreciate you letting me get a glimpse of Ziggy's life."

"Come on, let me show you what I've been working on. I know you have that modeling audition to get to." Ziggy took her arm and led her away. A quick glance over her shoulder told her Zeke was watching them still.

Ziggy led her to a terminal in the far corner in the last line of desks. He took a seat and booted the computer. She glanced at Zeke, relieved to find that he was talking to someone at a terminal and no longer concentrating on her.

"Listen. I need you to stay here or with a friend until I come back."

"How do I know you'll come back and this isn't just a trick?"

Sarah pulled up a chair next to his and sighed. "Until this is over, I need you to do something for me."

"Like is this part of my job?"

A half smile curled on her lips. "Sure. If I don't check in with you in the next twenty-four hours, it's because I've been compromised by those bad people that have my friend. It means they stopped me. If that happens, I want you to go public. I want you to..." She dug through the backpack until she found Ice Man's picture. "I want you to spam this picture every-where without letting up. I want you to drive this guy so far underground that he's deeper than anyone he's ever buried. I want you to spill everything you know. Can you and your friends do that?"

"Yeah, a piece of cake." His brows dipped. "Are they going to hurt you?"

"Maybe." Sarah swallowed. "But maybe not, if I tell them I have a backup plan."

"What's that?" he asked.

"You're my backup. Keep up, Ziggy," Sarah said.

His eyes widened as if he just now understanding the severity of her predicament. She took out Marvin Crenshaw's extra biofeed and clamped it to her ankle, turning it on where she stored the coordinates for future use before abruptly turning it back off. With the damage to the compound, she doubted that anyone would be scanning the GPS coordinates on the travelers especially since they were all corralled in Area 2.

"Let me see your phone," she said.

He did, and she pinged her contact information to his and his to hers. She rose and walked to the brick wall and held up her hand and turned her biofeed on. She stored the coordinates again as a backup.

"You can't just do that here." Ziggy jumped out of his seat.

"I'm not. I'm storing the information so I can come back. You know, if my phone dies."

"Right." The fine lines of Ziggy's face smoothed.

"Twenty-four hours, starting now," she said, and when Ziggy didn't move, she grabbed his hand and started the timer on his watch. "If you don't hear from me, you know what to do."

"Maybe you shouldn't do this?" His look turned to one of concern.

"If not me, who else will stop them?" She patted his back. "Twenty-four hours and be sure to cover your tracks if it comes to it. They already know where you live, so don't go home."

19

Sarah had no clue what she was walking into. She had a gun, cuffs, and a backup plan. Jonathan's secrecy and betrayal cut straight to her core. Her world spun like a tornado, leaving her dizzy in the wake of its chaos. The one person she needed and relied on to have her back was involved with the enemy.

She needed answers. Not only did she need to find Logan, Emma, and the Stillmans but she needed to figure out why they were in danger in the first place. Only a handful of people even knew they were here.

To figure out the motive, she needed to locate the time-hiding witnesses to question them. She had a starting point. The bridge in Central Park and the freighter at the docks. The bridge in Central Park just seemed like a gateway, so she'd bypass that one and go straight to the freighter. It was a secure location with a vantage point of being able to see everyone coming and going, everyone except for her.

Sarah didn't use her biofeed to get there; not to give Kemper new means of finding her. She did it the old-fashioned way by taking the subway as close to the docks as she could and grabbed a cab the rest of the way.

She stood on a roof of a nearby building for a better viewpoint of the dock and what was going on behind the gates. Seagulls circled the water and boats. Offshore fog rolled in on the breeze. It wouldn't be long before it would obstruct her view.

Cranes lifted and repositioned metal freight containers the size of small mobile homes. Workers in hard hats seemed oblivious to the danger near them. No guns in sight other than the ones the guards at the gate were holding.

"What's the plan? Go in guns blazing?" The sound of Foster's voice had her spinning around.

"How did you find me?"

He took her wrist and ran his finger over her pulse before unfastening the biofeed band from her arm. "I hacked your biofeed. It gave me your exact location."

"Can Kemper do that?" she asked.

"Who do you think taught me?" Foster took her biofeed and dropped it to the ground before smashing it with his boot.

"That must be how he followed me to Ziggy's apartment."

"Ziggy Carmichael?" Foster's brows dipped as he asked.

"Oh, now how in the hell do you know about Ziggy?"

"We should leave this location in case Kemper tracks you here." Foster took her by the arm and opened a portal, taking her back down to the alley, where he whisked her a few alleyways over before he stopped. "In the time I come from, Ziggy is an important person in your past."

"How—"

"It doesn't matter." He glanced out of the alleyway toward the docks. "So what's the plan?"

Sarah chewed her bottom lip.

"You don't have one?" Foster's voice deepened in confusion.

"I'd planned to go find them and get them out via my biofeed, but you just stomped my plans to the ground." Literally.

"I guess it's a good thing we have mine." He slipped his sleeve up his arm to show her.

"Aren't you worried that Ice Man will track you?" Sarah asked.

"Who?" He asked.

"Kemper."

"Oh, Ice Man…." Foster gestured to his hair. "…I

get it. But why would Kemper do that? He thinks I'm dead." Foster slipped his fingers through hers and guided her out of the alleyway. "Don't look so surprised. It's a long story better left for a rainy day."

They walked for a mile in silence down the loading dock, checking the perimeter of the fence until he found a spot that looked as though the fence was cut away from the pole and lifted out of the ground. He pulled the fence high and taut for her to slide beneath before he followed.

After she'd helped him up, they hurried behind a freight container. She swiped the dirt from her jeans before lifting her gaze to find him watching her. A smile and something akin to affection shown in his eyes.

"What?"

"What? What?" The smile slipped from his lips as he took her hand and began pulling her down and around aisles full of containers.

"Don't tell me that I'm important in your future too," she whispered when he stopped to peer at their surroundings.

"My future ended with my death. I have no idea what's in store for me."

"I bet that makes it confusing. If you ever got sent back, you'd have a lot of explaining to do."

"I don't plan to go back."

"Okay, then why were you smiling like you had a secret?"

Panic filled his eyes as he pulled her against his chest and out of sight around the back of a container. His hand covered her mouth. Her heart raced as her eyes followed the direction he was looking.

He waited a few more seconds before he released his hand. "You're an enigma in my time. Like a campfire fairytale told to little girls and boys to scare them."

"I'm a monster in the future?" Sarah asked. "That's… creepy."

"You're like a ghost. If anyone steps out of line, they say, 'The Weston will get you.' They have a whole nursery rhyme about you."

Sarah's lips twisted at the corners. "You're kidding me."

He shrugged and took her hand, easing his gaze around the edge of the container. He pulled her into a jog through the maze.

"How do you know which container to look inside?"

"I already know," he answered.

"How?" she asked.

"The same way I found you," he said, pointing to the biofeed.

She pulled him to a stop. "That's not possible. Logan tossed me his biofeed, Emma didn't have one, and Doc Stillman's went offline, along with his wife's."

"You're under the assumption that the biofeed

GPS is the only way we can track someone in the future." He grinned, pulling her into a fast walk.

He clicked a few buttons on his unique biofeed, and a blue light pulsated on the screen. "I have a setting that tracks disturbance and energy usage around me. It was incorporated in the future to help travelers always know where they can find their nearest energy source for an easy exit. It's similar to locating a battery outlet."

"And you think we'll find that here? If Ziggy followed these guys here, then no way did they do it through a time slip. They had to travel the old-fashioned way."

"Just because they didn't travel that way doesn't mean they can't. Water is an energy conductor, and with the right tools, it can be harnessed to create the blue light you use in your transponder room." He glanced at her. "Why do you think so many people and vehicles go missing in the Bermuda Triangle?"

He took a step, and she stopped him. "You can't mean that those missing people, boats, and aircraft arrived somewhere else and are living in another time?"

"That's exactly what I mean. How do you think it's possible no debris is ever recovered, even with the notion that large scary waves are taking these vessels down?" He stared down at the energy tracker function on his biofeed.

He turned on the spot watching the energy meter fluctuate until he turned back toward a cargo ship where the meter pegged at maximum energy. He pointed. "They have a setup in there."

20

"We could swim and shimmy up the port bow," he suggested.

Her stomach rolled and beads of sweat dotted her forehead as she stared down at the dark murky water below. "Swimming isn't an option."

He gestured down the dock. "We could get in at that point. It wouldn't take five minutes, and we'd be undetected."

"It's not an option because I can't swim," she whispered.

"You're serious?" he asked.

"My mom spent a lot of time in the labs. I didn't have a normal childhood growing up. Where other kids went to school, I had scientists teaching me everything I needed to know."

"What about friends?" he asked.

She cleared her throat. "That's not relevant." She

gestured to the plank, which was the only way to get on the boat. "We'll wait until dark."

He noted the GPS coordinates where they were standing and recorded them. "Come on, we've got some time to kill. Let's feed you."

He punched in some coordinates on his biofeed, and a living room appeared on the other side. She stepped inside to find the room, complete with a fireplace and a nice-sized open kitchen.

Blinds covered the window, blocking her view. "Where are we?"

"My home," he announced, tossing his biofeed onto the counter and rubbing his wrist. He walked into the kitchen. "What can I get you to drink?"

"Nothing, I'm fine," she answered.

"Nonsense," he said, starting the coffee pot. Within minutes he'd poured her a cup and added her favorite creamer in just the right amount.

"How a person takes their coffee is personal," she said, taking it from him and sipping the warm concoction. She moaned around the rich flavor. "You made my cup like you've done it a thousand times before."

He smiled but didn't answer her. Instead, he grabbed a beer from the fridge and popped the top before grabbing a casserole dish full of what looked to be a dish of already cooked lasagna from the refrigerator and popping it into the oven to heat it up. He set the timer for 30 minutes. "If I didn't know any better, I'd think you knew we'd have time to kill."

He grinned again. "Come on, let me show you the something." He grabbed a remote and pushed buttons. The surrounding blinds opened, revealing an astonishing view of the northern lights. Colors danced across the vast open sky in a stream full of never-ending color, like a kaleidoscope that ebbed and flowed from one color to the next. A smile slid onto her lips. For as many secrets that she was privy to, it was the same secrets that isolated her. It was places like this where her own curiosity and awe for nature reminded her how many secrets she still needed to learn. This beautiful canvas proved it.

"You approve," he said, coming to stand next to her.

"It's stunning, but I thought you lived with Charlie."

"I do." His smile slipped. "I mean, I look in on him, and I'm there for him daily, but this place… this is my own little sanctuary."

"How did you come to buy this place when you're supposed to be dead? It had to have cost you a fortune."

"Knowing the future has a lot of perks." He smiled.

"Tell me you didn't break one of the agency's rules by changing the luck of someone who was supposed to win the lottery."

"Um… not quite. I told you that I used to be on Kemper's team."

"And…." she asked.

"Well, I may have put a bug into someone's ear to stop Kemper from changing the future."

"Well, if that's not cryptic."

"Let's just say, this isn't the only assignment Adam Kemper and I worked."

Sarah turned back to admire the lights. The less she knew, the better. Plausible deniability, kind of like how the sister agency was keeping secrets from the government. They were the same way. Don't ask, don't tell.

That was where she had problems. Sarah had to know. It was deep-rooted in her DNA. And if she did know, then she would worry about it for all eternity. The not knowing, the being out of the loop was what gave her heart palpitations.

"What does Charlie know about the witnesses?"

"Not much. They were all brought in under very guarded circumstances. Only the head of the FBI and the person running the labs were giving the information."

Sarah needed to find a way into Richard's office or figure out where he or his mother, who preceded him in the position, would keep classified files. She had the names and the faces, but not their backstory, which would help her figure out what all of this was about.

The timer dinged, pulling her attention from her thoughts. Foster set the table and plated the food like they were on a first date. Sarah couldn't shake the urgency that skirted her spine; the need to go ahead and charge onto the boat to end things once and for all.

She took a bite and glanced up at the clock on the wall. Her twenty-four hours was dwindling.

They bantered about his experience in this time. He'd let a few things slip like the future state of the economy and air quality and a few notions of how different things in his time compared to now.

An hour went by. The night turned darker, and she was pacing the floor and kept checking the clock. "We should go now."

"It's too soon."

"What if the boat leaves? What if they move everyone? We need to go now."

"Always so anxious. Some things never change." Foster rose from his spot and set down his beer. He slid his gun into a holster attached to the waistband of his jeans.

"You have your gun?" he asked.

She nodded. "Let's go."

He opened a time slip at the docks, and they both stepped through. The night was darker at the docks compared to where they'd viewed the aurora borealis. No guards were monitoring the gangway or roaming the deck. It was quiet aside from the water slapping against the boats and dock.

The ghostly atmosphere and quietness of their

surroundings prickled the hair on her neck. "Does this seem too easy?"

He slipped his gun free and held it pointed at the ground. "Yep. Keep your guard up."

She crouched down and followed behind him onto the boat, feeling a bit more at ease when she had her back pressed against a wall. He tapped on his biofeed and led the way toward the blinking blue light where the electromagnetic rangefinder was off the charts. He peered through the door and turned back to her. "Son of a…" He moved out of her way so she could peer inside. "Kemper found some witnesses. They're being held in an energy holding cell."

Logan was lying on a bed. Emma, Doc Stillman, and his wife were inside the same cell. There was one guard in a chair across the room. Butterflies the size of bats swarmed in unease inside her stomach.

"Let me get the guard before you rush in," Foster announced, disappearing the way they'd come.

He appeared across the room at another opening where the guard had his back toward the door. Foster put him in a chokehold and they tussled until the guard slunk unconsciously down to the floor and out of Foster's grasp.

Sarah pulled her gun and entered the room. They both hurried over to the energy cell. Logan's face was drained of color. Confusion clouded Dr. Stillman's brow as he rose and pushed his wife behind him.

"What the hell are you doing here?"

Sarah stepped into view. "It's okay. We're here to rescue you."

Stillman's brows dipped in even more contention as the energy cell lowered and Foster opened a portal. "I'll explain everything later. Get Logan and your wife and go."

Sarah recognized the location. Charlie's basement, where she and Foster had first arrived.

Dr. Stillman grabbed Logan and tossed him over his shoulder as his wife and Emma stepped through the portal ahead of him. He was about to cross the threshold, and Sarah would have been next, when she heard Jonathan's voice.

"Drop your weapon or die."

Sarah spun to find Foster's gun aimed at her head. Her brows dipped in confusion as he grabbed her around the waist and held the gun to her head.

"Foster, what the hell are you doing?"

He didn't answer, only tapped the portal closed. He pulled her backward out of another door toward the deck as she fought his hold.

"Stop struggling, Sarah, or I'll kill Jonathan first and let you watch. You have no idea what ramifications that would have on history." Foster chuckled in her ear.

Everything after that happened in an instant. Foster had backed her up to the edge of the boat. A portal opened alongside him to what looked like the inside of Ziggy's apartment.

Jonathan aimed his gun at Foster's head. Jonathan's gaze strayed to Sarah's face before settling back on Foster.

"Sarah told me a secret. She can't swim. Has she told you that yet?" Foster asked. "You have a choice to make, Jonathan. Save Sarah or catch me."

Foster stepped through the portal and shoved Sarah over the boat railing into a free fall. A shot rang out seconds before Sarah hit the water, knocking all the air from her lungs.

She flailed, kicking her arms and legs, trying to reach the moonlight above until the last spec of light floated away behind her closing eyes. Her lungs burned, and her body jerked as the ocean water replaced the air in her lungs and the last bit of breath escaped her body.

21

S arah gasped. Her eyes flew open as she rolled to her side and coughed water from her lungs in an uncontrollable fit until there was nothing left of the dark murky water in her body. She rolled onto her back to find Jonathan leaning over her. A look of relief eased his worry creases.

Sarah's eyes slid closed once again, leading her into a darkened abyss where even the coldness of her body refused to keep her awake.

She didn't know how long she'd been out when she finally woke inside an unfamiliar room. Jonathan was staring down at her.

"You're awake." Relief filled his words.

"Where are we?" She asked glancing around in the large empty room that only had a few pieces of medical equipment. Her body swayed with the motion as she glanced down at the large oversized shirt covering her body. "And what the hell am I wearing?"

"You're still on the boat and your clothes were soaked, so I changed you into one of my shirts. Your jeans are dry now though." He answered gesturing to the end of the bed.

"About damn time," Kemper growled as he entered the room. "We need to know where Foster is."

Sarah slowly pushed herself up in the bed, letting the memories return of what actually had taken place. "I don't understand. I thought he was the good guy and you two were bad."

"You thought I went to the dark side?" Jonathan's brows dipped asked unable to hide the hurt of Sarah's accusation.

"Ziggy showed me a picture of you, Kemper, and his team in Central Park. What did you expect me to think? Foster said that Kemper was trying to kill the witnesses."

"Witnesses?"

"Emma, Dr. Stillman, and his wife."

Jonathan let out a tired breath. "I told you we should have brought her into the loop. We could have stopped all of this days ago."

"It was need to know, and she didn't need to know," Kemper growled.

"She thinks they were innocents. Be glad she didn't shoot you to protect them," Jonathan said, sitting down on the bed. He met her gaze again. "Sarah, they aren't witnesses. They're sleeper cells. They're orchestrating futuristic outcomes by planning and making arrangements years in advance. Like a war that I've been told will take place. There is now a nuclear bomb missing along with codes. We believe Emma orchestrated it."

She slowly shook her head. Her chest felt like it was caving in. "You're wrong. I've seen their faces, their files. They helped bring down a future dictator. Charlie…"

"Dr. Claremont?" Adam asked.

"Yeah. He told me they're hiding here and that the head of the FBI and the labs are the only ones who know their secrets."

"But you've seen their faces?" he asked.

"Yes," she answered.

"He was part of the execution in the future. It was his brainchild. Foster was supposed to help me stop Dr. Claremont, but somehow he must have been turned or tainted to their side. We tried to tell you when we searched for Ziggy."

That explained the money and the house with the view. Sarah's shoulders sagged. She grabbed her phone on the table to find it soaked and unworkable.

"Ziggy," Sarah screeched and checked her watch. She had fifteen minutes left of her twenty-four hours. "We have to stop him."

Jonathan rested his arm on hers to calm her as she reached for her jeans. "Stop him from what?"

Sarah jumped out of the bed and slid the jeans up her legs, fastening the buttons before shoving her feet into her shoes she found by the bed. "Exposing you and Adam. If I don't check in within twenty-four hours, the time program will be made public, along with the picture of you and Adam being criminals."

Jonathan and Adam exchanged a look. "I told you she was good."

"Go, and take Jonathan with you. We'll meet back at Area 2. Dr. Richard Bay has some explaining to do." Kemper handed her a biofeed, and she was quick to punch in the last coordinates she'd memorized. Jonathan stepped through the portal with her, and they ended up in an alley near the dumpster that blocked the path into the old subway system. She pushed it out of the way with his help, and they both descended the stairs.

She ran with him following behind her until they reached where voices were arguing.

All the talking stopped as she stepped into view.

"She's here. She made it back," Zeke said.

"But she's with him. He's the bad guy," Ziggy announced.

Sarah held up her hands. "He's not the bad guy. It was all a misunderstanding."

"You told Ziggy Carmichael that I was the bad guy?" Jonathan gawked.

"A lot has happened since we apprehended Marvin."

"If he's not the bad guy, then who is?" Ziggy asked.

"Foster, but I don't even know if that's his real name," she said.

"You got his picture? We can ruin that guy's day," Zeke offered.

"No, but thanks, guys," Jonathan announced, taking her by the arm and ushering her to leave.

"Wait," Ziggy called out. "You're supposed to take me with you."

"Seriously, Sarah?" Jonathan growled.

"He's important to me in the future unless Foster lied about that too."

"She offered me a job."

Jonathan's eyes bulged, and a look of disbelief crossed his face. She patted his chest. "It will be easier to watch him this way. Come on, Ziggy, we've got some work to do."

They emerged into the alleyway, and Jonathan opened a portal inside the agency building.

The building smelled like smoke, but most of the pit area where the analysts worked was still intact if not a little broken. Computers were being replaced as company employees helped each other to right the wrongs that had occurred.

Sarah and Jonathan headed toward the elevators

as Ziggy was turning in the spot, awkwardly introducing himself to everyone around him. Sarah grabbed him by the arm and pulled him into the elevator. "They already know who you are."

"That is so cool," he cooed like a kid that knows Santa's secret identity. She hit the button for the top floor and glared at him. "This is not training class. This is real life-or-death problems, so don't speak, don't ask questions, and just keep quiet and out of our way until this situation is under control. Understood?"

Ziggy made like he was zipping his lips and turned his gaze to the climbing number.

When the elevator dinged, he followed them off and straight into Dr. Richard Bay's office, bypassing Carol's empty desk.

Richard was sitting behind his computer, his fingers frantically pounding the keyboard only slowing as they entered the room.

"Dick, we know you're in on it. Your family was responsible for the sleepers," Sarah announced.

"What the hell are you talking about?"

"You know about the sleeper agents put in our time trying to change history."

"How dare you accuse me of being a part of any of this?"

"Kemper and Jonathan told me."

"You have no proof," he growled turning his chair to face her, as she rounded his desk.

Sarah slammed her foot onto the chair. He was quick to open his legs protecting his crotch with his hands. She shoved the chair across the room with him in it so she could get access to his desk.

"What the hell are you doing?"

"You're right, we need proof, and I'm betting it's in your office. You and your mother were meticulous record keepers. It's why I got along with you both. Always so anal." Sarah yanked open one of the drawers, grabbed the contents and dumped everything onto the desk. She did the same with the rest.

"You're a shame to your mother's memory." Richard's voice was dark, making her pause.

"That's debatable," Kemper said, stepping inside the room.

Her mother. Sarah walked over to the honored employees on the wall, which included her mother's face. She glanced over her shoulder back at him. "Was it true my mother was in this program?"

He didn't answer as Sarah took her mother's picture off the wall. If Foster was right, then she was a sleeper too. Was that what got her killed?

"Sorry." Ziggy moved to stand by her. "Is that your mom?"

"What did I tell you, Ziggy?" Sarah growled.

"I know. It's just that I've seen that woman."

"Where?" they all asked him in unison, catching him off guard.

"On my tenth birthday at my mom's house. She

brought me a birthday present. She told me that one day it would make sense and to keep the present safe until it does. She told me she was a time traveler." Ziggy's gaze cleared. "She's the reason I've been searching for proof my entire life."

22

"What did she give you?" Sarah asked, setting the picture of her mother on the pile of files on the desk.

Ziggy's gaze followed her mom's face, and his brows dipped. He pointed to the picture. He pointed to a blue stone around her mother's neck. "She gave me that." He shoved some files out of his way. "In a box that looks that that."

The circular box on the desk had always been there. Sarah could remember it when she and her mother used to visit the Labs. A compass was etched into the wood surface.

Jonathan tried to pick it up, and it wouldn't budge, as if it were soldered to the desk. He squatted to be eye level with it and ran his fingers around the groove.

"It's not a box. It looks like a knob." He said,

twisting the compass until he heard a click and the Northern point was aimed at the wall across the room.

"Don't touch that." Richard growled and tried to rise again.

Kemper pushed him back down in his seat. "Just sit there and shut up. You're already in enough trouble."

The wall started to move revealing a secret room, with pictures of the sleepers with their real identities beneath each. A machine like the quantum computer was in the middle of the room. Sarah stepped into the room, and it lit up.

"Analyst Sarah Weston, daughter of Jane Weston, identity activated."

"What the hell?" Richard gasped, rising from his seat. "How is it programmed for you and not for me? I've been trying for years to get that damn thing to work."

Sarah glanced over her shoulder and grinned. "Everyone knows my adoptive mother was a brilliant scientist and analyst, but few know she was an extremely capable hacker."

She rested her hand on the reader much like the one she used to get her reports from the quantum computer. This computer momentarily came to life before slowly dying like it ran out of battery.

Insert power source, flashed on the screen.

Sarah was running her hand over the grooves on

the podium when Ziggy stepped up beside her. "You know what it needs?"

She grinned and glanced up at him. "Yep, but unfortunately, I don't have time to test our theory. I have a terrorist to catch."

They'd both stepped out of the secret room and back into the office area when the office door burst open, banging off the wall behind it. Diana hurried into the room carrying her computer. "I've hacked into Dr. Bay's home computer, Sarah, and you'll never guess what I found," she said before her gaze caught the secret room. "Cool."

"That's what I said," Ziggy announced.

"Focus, people," Jonathan warned. "What did you find?"

"Jonathan asked me to look into the Bays' financials, starting with his mother. I found ten million dollars in deposits into a family trust with different names and account numbers associated with each of them. I found the accompanying ledger on his computer. It was encrypted, but I cracked the code."

Dr. Bay was reaching for Diana when Kemper threw him back in his chair and pointed a gun at his head. "Continue."

"Your mom gave them money, Sarah, and was listed as a contributor. Only next to her name was the word Mole and then Deceased."

Sarah lunged for Dr. Bay on the other side of the desk, and Jonathan grabbed her and pulled her back against his chest. The need to get her fingers around his throat and choke the life from his body had her heart racing. He knew more than what he was saying. He knew more, and she would stop at nothing to make him confess.

"A dead man isn't any good to us," Jonathan whispered into her ear.

"You killed my mother!" Sarah screamed.

"That traitor should have died a slower death, and if my mother had her choice, you would have been with her."

Sarah struggled to get out of Jonathan's hold, and his hold tightened.

"Whose idea was it to keep her alive?" Jonathan asked.

"You should know," Richard growled. "She talked you into finally telling her how you feel."

Sarah's brows furrowed. "What the hell is he talking about?"

"I was going to tell you that night in the cabin." His brows dipped, and he frowned.

"Tell me what?" she asked.

"That I wanted you and me to be together. Sarah…you know how I feel."

"This isn't the time for that, people," Kemper announced.

"Sarah, your mom talked me into taking you to the cabin. She said you loved it there. She wanted me to pull out all the stops to help you take a chance on me. It was her idea. She wanted you to find happiness. I think she was worried if anything happened to her that you'd be left all alone."

"You never told me," Sarah whispered. "I was supposed to be in the car with her. I was supposed to drive her that night. If I'd been there, she might still be alive."

"For a day, a week, a month, maybe, Sarah, but they would have eventually got to her. Your mother was never a sleeper," Kemper announced. "She was always working for the good guys. She had some important information to tell us. It was her idea to meet at the beach house since you weren't with her."

"She never made it," Sarah answered for him.

"No." Adam visibly swallowed before his eyes flashed in anger. "She never did."

"Put Richard in holding. We have to go to Claremont's house to see if the sleepers are still there."

Richard's gaze went to one of the pictures on the wall, and Sarah followed his stare. Only the picture on the wall and the name didn't match. "That's not the Charles I met."

Richard's lips twisted into a smile.

23

S arah and the others stepped out of the portal into Charles Claremont's kitchen. It had been the only place she'd tagged with her GPS. The kitchen was quiet; the entire house was. It was eerily quiet. Everyone fanned out in different directions. Sarah knew exactly where she wanted to look.

"Be careful," Jonathan's voice was a whisper in her ear comm.

"Copy that. I'm going to search the lab in the basement." Sarah kept her finger on the trigger as she traversed the maze she'd traversed once before with Foster.

The comm in her ear clicked to life with acknowledgement each time someone cleared a room. They worked in unison like a well-oiled machine.

She opened the basement door and took a tentative step, quiet and calculating she descended the stairs, one at time, cringing with each creak. She hit bottom and spun in place, pointing her gun in each direction while listening for any sounds.

Shallow breathing. A voice so faint she couldn't tell whose it was much less hear the words. "Help me."

Sarah eased around the corner into the open room where Dr. Claremont had once stood on his podium. The room was empty except for the bleeding body lying propped up on one of the concrete columns.

"Logan," she whispered and dropped to her knees. His eyes closed, and she clutched his face. "Stay with me, Logan."

His eyes opened again. "They said you'd come. She played me, Sarah. I'm so sorry."

"She played us all, Logan."

Logan's head lolled again.

Sarah pressed the comm in her ear. "Logan is in the basement. He needs the infirmary."

Logan lifted his hand to rest on her arm, his eyes trying to focus on her. "He was waiting on you."

Her brows dipped. "Dr. Claremont?"

He patted her hand that held the gun and glanced toward another door she hadn't noticed before. "Foster."

"You hold on, okay?" she whispered.

He slowly nodded before she made her way to the door, carefully easing it open. She descended stairs into an underground tunnel. The overhead lights were dim and built into the stone. She started in a jog, coming out into a wooded area behind the house. She scanned the trees for movement, and she spotted him. He smiled at her and turned to run. She took off like the hounds of hell were chasing her. No way was she letting him get away. Not now.

"I'm headed into the woods." She yelled for everyone to hear in their ear comms. Sarah pumped her arms and her legs, jumping over a fallen tree limb like it was a mere hurdle and she was in the Olympics. Her lungs burned as she pushed herself harder and harder until she reached a clearing with a time slip still open.

She ran for it and jumped inside, only slowing to figure out where in the hell he'd taken her.

She appeared inside a museum exhibit in the belly of a fake cave portraying how cavemen lived. She stepped out and found a kid staring at her. His mouth parted as if words failed him. Sarah stepped out of the exhibit. "Did you see a man come through here?"

She glanced at the flier in the kid's hand.

He nodded and pointed down a hall labeled Observatory.

"New York Museum Observatory," she whispered seconds before throwing the observatory door open and letting the light shine into a darkened room where stars lit the ceiling like space itself. She took a minute to let her eyes adjust as she started walking, scanning each individual until she'd almost reached the other door.

Arms banded around her with one covering her mouth and the other across her waist. She was pulled against a hard chest. She didn't have to see his face to know who was holding her. His familiar scent was her only clue.

"I knew you'd come," he whispered as she struggled out of his hold. "I waited. I told them you were too stubborn to fail catching me." He inhaled the scent along the column of her neck. "You're wearing my favorite perfume."

She continued to struggle to try and get out of his hold.

"I wasn't supposed to lead you away from the fireworks."

Her eyes widened in surprise as fear strung every nerve in her body.

"Don't worry. There's still time to save them all… well, hopefully all." He pulled her farther away from the spectators watching the stars and out of sight into a smaller observation room attached.

He pushed the biofeed on her arm and opened a portal just outside the safe house where they'd met.

"I gave Jonathan the same choice. He chose wrong. Ask him who saved you. Who pulled you out of the water." His breath was hot against her cheek. "You need me as much as I need you, Sarah."

He slowly lowered his hand when she started mumbling into his fingers.

"You're right. I need you…" Her gaze searched the dim room until it landed on the twinkle of metal. "…to die." She closed her eyes and cringed. "Copy that. Take the shot."

The whiz of a bullet sounded out seconds before she felt the impact and burn as it tore through her arm and into Foster standing behind her. He dropped his hold of her before falling into the portal, holding the blood oozing from his chest. Jonathan stepped out of the shadows and in front of the portal. He pointed his gun again but didn't have time to get off another shot before the portal closed.

"Now aren't you glad you're wearing your comm?" Jonathan asked Sarah as he studied the wound where the bullet pierced her arm.

"You shot me," she whispered.

"I saved you," he replied.

"By shooting me?" she asked.

"I shot him, too, if it makes you feel any better," Jonathan said, helping her stand. He dialed in a portal to open back at the lab.

"It doesn't make me feel any better and besides you missed. You should have went for the head."

Jonathan's lifted his gaze from her arm to her eyes. "I couldn't chance accidently missing and killing you."

"Wait, he said there was a bomb." She tried to wiggle free from his hold.

"We found it and disabled it. Everyone is out, including the real Dr. Charles Claremont. He has a ton to tell you, by the way, and is looking forward to meeting you."

They stepped through the portal just outside the lab. The sun was just starting to rise over the horizon. The adrenaline she'd been running on had drained from her body. Every step seemed like a monumental task.

Sarah rested her hand on the wall. "I need to rest."

Jonathan lifted her up into his arms and started toward the temporary infirmary. "You're such a slacker, Weston, but don't worry, I've got you."

24

S arah, Ziggy, and the real Doctor Claremont stood in the hidden room in Dr. Richard Bay's old office. Sarah and the others had found the real doctor bound and gagged in a locked room when they'd breached the house. His role in overseeing the labs until a replacement could be brought in would be an invaluable resource.

Ziggy slid the blue-orbed pendant into the grooves. They shared an excited look as Sarah placed her palm into the reader and the room filled with light and life.

A map of the continents filled the screen, two blinking blue lights in the United States. Sarah maneuvered the map to focus on the location. Both were in New York, located in different places across town.

"What do you suppose those are?" Ziggy asked, standing next to Sarah at the computer.

She didn't know how to answer him. She had no clue what they might indicate.

"Those are tears in the fabric of time. Time slips that were opened and never closed. We called them entrance points or backdoors," Dr. Claremont said from the back of the room.

Entrance Points glowed on the map, pinned to portals that had been jammed open as if someone had propped a chair against them so they wouldn't close.

"Why would you need a back door?" Sarah asked.

"Think like a hacker, Sarah. Backdoors are ways to sneak in undetected," Ziggy answered.

"We can't leave them open. Something deadly might walk through, not to mention we have to figure out the reason for the tears in the first place. How do we close them?" she asked Dr. Claremont.

"I'm not sure. When I was here, the lab didn't have anything in our arsenal that could close the slips, but that might have changed in the years I've been gone," Dr. Claremont said. "We'll have to make solving this problem our priority."

Two days later, when Sarah sent a crew to the sites to research the area, they found three dead bodies, including the two sleepers, Emma and Dr. Stillman's wife. They'd been responsible for opening the portals. Their blue pendants they'd been wearing around their neck in their arrival pictures were gone.

Dr. Stillman's body was found with his wife's. The people that held the information they needed were dying. Their usefulness was over. Their mission was done.

With the blue pendant Sarah's mother had given Ziggy for safekeeping, there was one less entry point they'd need to worry about, even though there were several sleepers still unaccounted for and missing. The mystery of why Sarah's mom had given the pendant to Ziggy in the first place would have to remain unanswered, but if Sarah had to guess, her mother had been three steps ahead of everyone else and this wasn't over by a long shot. Sarah had faith, her mother's reasons would eventually come to light.

With a little ingenuity and the help of the news, they'd plastered the IDs and faces of the dead sleepers for the other sleepers to see. Giving them a heads-up on what fate awaited them would buy Sarah's organization a little more time to catch Foster and the fake Dr. Claremont, whose name she now knew was Dr. Stephen Steed.

Dr. Richard Bay had been detained until the Deputy Director of the FBI had shown up to cart him away to someplace more suited to keeping him under lock and key. The court system hadn't had a need for laws against manipulating time, but judging by the way things were going, they'd need to implement some soon. The only secretive governing body was the Time Magistrate and Kemper was in the process of escorting Marvin Crenshaw to answer for what he'd almost accomplished.

Thanks to the pictures that Sarah had taken, faces of all the sleepers and their handlers now lined the wall in the pit. Agents would be working around the clock to locate them along with Steed and Foster. They had a starting point. All they needed was one sleeper to reveal the secrets on how to close the portals and life as they knew it would get back to normal.

Sarah sat in the dark, staring through the glass at the blue light in the transponder room. Her computer was running a facial recognition on all of the faces in an attempt to find them and put a stop to it all.

The sweet smell of French pastries drifted to Sarah's nose, pulling her from her thoughts. Sarah spun around to find Jonathan holding up to-go containers from the restaurant she'd asked him about on the way to pick up Crenshaw.

"You finally pulled the trigger and went on your date to the restaurant? So who was the lucky girl?"

"You are." Jonathan grinned as he took the seat at the desk across from hers. He held out the container and a fork.

She took both, not wasting any time before digging in. "Even the French do take-out."

He chuckled as her gaze landed on the reports that Diana had pulled for her. With the reports of Marvin's biofeed GPS, which she'd been wearing around her ankle, and Jonathan's side by side, her heart sank into her stomach when she realized that Foster had been right. Jonathan had chosen wrong. At the exact moment Sarah inhaled salt water, Jonathan's biofeed had taken him elsewhere, away from saving her and not arriving until five minutes later.

She still had no idea who had pulled her out of the water; she just knew who it wasn't.

"Why the sad face? I thought sweets would perk you up."

Sarah moved her GPS report over Jonathan's and smiled, ignoring the worry in her mind. "I'm not sad. How can anyone be sad eating this?"

She shoved another bite into her mouth and moaned, even though she didn't taste a thing. She relaxed into her chair, trying as she might to let the tension drain from her face. She didn't want to think about the GPS comparisons. She didn't want to think that Jonathan had left her to die. She wanted things to go back to the way they were.

While eating he'd teased her about having to train Ziggy. "He's going to be a pain in the ass."

"No different than when you and I trained together," she teased back.

"Do you think he's going to try to blab about all of this in his internet videos?"

"No, not now that he knows the truth, but if he ever does, then I'll stop him." She sighed. It was times like these she'd missed talking and working out solutions with Jonathan. No matter how many times her gaze strayed to the reports, she silently wondered just who was playing whom. Jonathan hung out with her for about thirty minutes. It seemed he missed their easy banter as much as she did.

When he left, Sarah rubbed her tired eyes before locking up the GPS reports in her desk. She headed back into her newly assigned temporary room since hers had been impacted by the explosion. She didn't like sleeping at the facility, but she would tonight. She used her biofeed to unlock the door and stepped into the sparse room.

The smell of Italian herbs smacked her in the face. A smell she knew well, the same smell from the lasagna Foster had made her. Sarah grabbed her gun and had it pointing at the ground as she rounded the foyer into the living room-dining room combo.

The rooms were empty. She cleared her bedroom and the bathroom, even checking behind the shower curtain, before the tension slowly started to ease from her shoulders.

Sitting on her breakfast bar was a plastic container. She opened the container to find it was the lasagna that Foster had made her. She took the container and dumped it into the trash for fear he'd somehow drugged it. Foster was nothing if not inventive. Her phone rang at that exact moment. She answered on the third ring.

"Sarah, you miss me yet?" Foster said.

"How did you get this new number?" she asked, dropping her gaze to the bar. She clenched her eyes closed.

"I have my ways," he answered. "I left you dinner and a movie."

"This isn't some date," she growled. "Tell me how to close the time slips."

"All in good time," he teased. "You're going to want to watch that movie, Sarah, and after you do, destroy the disk. It could get both of us killed. I only wish I was there to watch it with you."

Sarah lifted her gaze and spun in the direction of the DVD player. Sitting on top was a movie case that she hadn't put there. Sarah grabbed the DVD case and opened it while the phone was still pressed to her ear.

"Your mother would be disappointed that you threw away a perfectly good dinner. I'll be seeing you, Weston." The line disconnected, and she glared around the room, looking for cameras. She grabbed the disk and opened her biofeed to her beach house, an untainted place that only three people, one being her dead mother, knew Sarah liked to stay.

After pouring a glass of wine, she shoved the DVD into her player and clicked Play.

Sarah forgot to breathe as she watched the two women in a kitchen with their back to the camera.

"Turn around," she whispered to herself as she reached behind her for a chair before her legs gave out. "Turn around."

There was no sound on the video, just the women who looked like they were baking something. The second one turned around, Sarah froze the frame, and the glass of wine slipped from her fingers as she recognized her old assistant that everyone thought was dead. "Natalie."

She crawled to the TV screen with the remote in hand. She hit play and moved it frame by frame when the other woman turned around. "Mom."

How old was this? Where had Foster gotten it? All kinds of questions assaulted her mind as she took her time watching the short movie frame by frame. She paused when they moved the lasagna to the kitchen table.

Sarah's hand flew to cover her mouth. All reasonable thought and questions fluttered from her mind. The newspaper sitting on the table was the one from two days ago, an article about the mysterious deaths and pictures of the dead sleeper cells were on the front page.

She vowed then that she'd track Foster down to the ends of the earth and get him to spill everything he knew—by any means necessary.

KEEP READING for the first chapter of Time Keepers (Book 2 in the Sarah Weston Time Saga)

TIME KEEPERS

Sarah Weston punched buttons on the seemingly harmless watch on her wrist. To the unwitting onlooker, the electronic timepiece with the wide band looked like a high-priced watch. There was nothing too fancy about the apparatus. The band wasn't made out of gold, and there certainly weren't diamond inlays on the face. Nothing unusual to the untrained eye, but with the new systematic eye contact she was wearing on a test run, it powered the smorgasbord of information that was filling her vision like a computer screen. The contact interface lit up the streets and pedestrians around her like a computer game, complete with a digital trail of where her target was headed. All she had to do was follow the energy signature and its trail.

She took off running again, shoving and jostling her way through the Thanksgiving Day parade crowd.

Music blared as floats and displays inched by. Men, women, and children lined the street, as did police officers and other emergency personnel.

Sarah followed the red trail at a jog, only slowing when cops started watching her as if she were one of the mad men she was chasing. The second they looked away, she'd start running again. She almost missed the energy trail as it turned down an alley. She bounced off a red brick building as she maneuvered the turn into an alley. The alley was littered with more than just trash. An unsavory group of street thugs were huddled together as if discussing what score they were about to make.

The muscles in her shoulders tightened into knots as she stomped in their direction. Her hand lay on the gun beneath her jacket as she scanned their faces, letting the computer read their profiles to her through the comm in her ear. One by one their police file filled her vision until she figured out who was the baddest of them all. The ringleader. If she was going to make this quick, she had to go straight to the top and go for the throat.

Carlos Mateo scanned her from head to toe as she came to a stop in front of the group, his gaze assessing, no more than hers had been moments ago.

"I don't want any trouble. I'm just passing through."

"You turned down the wrong alley," he announced

as he slid a gun from the waist of his jeans and held it pointing to the ground.

The others with him grinned in sleazy sneers that they agreed.

"I don't care what you scum are up to. You aren't my target," she announced, holding her hands out to the side. Sarah didn't need a weapon to take on these five thugs. Even if they did get the drop on her, she'd walk away with barely a scratch. "A man ran down this alley five minutes ago. It's him I'm after."

The four other thugs started to fan out around her, blocking the path.

"I'll show you what a real man is." Carlos gave a little nod to one of the thugs, and Sarah turned her trained eye on him. His threat popped up first, a bulge from the knife beneath his coat, before the computer flashed the problem with his knee. That was the only in she needed.

She struck with the full force of her weight, breaking his leg in two. He went down fast and screaming, landing with a thud on his side as he held the broken limb in place.

Sarah pulled her gun and waved it between the remaining four. "Mateo, call them off. I'm just passing through."

"How do you know my name?" Mateo swaggered forward like he refused to be scared that a woman like her would be able to take him down.

Her brows dipped as his police file scanned in her

vision. It stopped on Mateo's police report filed on 911.

She flicked the safety off and cocked the trigger. "It doesn't matter how I know your name. What matters is that you're standing in the way of me catching a terrorist. Unless you want another 911, I suggest you let me pass."

"Kill that bitch," the man on the ground yelled just as Mateo lowered his weapon.

"Let her pass."

"Mateo, you see what she did to me."

"Yeah, she'll do the same if not worse to the terrorist. Let her pass." He slowly nodded and growled his order with vengeance. He waved his gun to the fire escape. "He took the stairs to the roof."

Sarah glanced up to find Foster smiling down on her. Aggravation seeped through her core. He held the answers she needed. She wouldn't stop until she either caught him or she was dead.

She hurried up the rungs of the ladder. The muscles in her legs already ached from the three-mile chase, yet she pushed through the pain and jumped onto the roof.

Before she could even grab her gun, she spotted Foster stepping into another time slip. She ran to follow him, barely making it before it closed.

She couldn't stop her momentum. Throwing her hands up, she bounced off a wall, smacking her head against the drywall. She fell backwards, hitting the ground with a thud. Her heart raced as she tried to catch her breath, staring up at a ceiling of a warehouse where a sky was painted on the ceiling. The lights flickered seconds before going out and another light turned on. The sky lit up with streams of colors like the aurora borealis, dancing back and forth across her vision.

"I'm not a bad guy, Sarah. Just a man between and rock and a hard spot."

"I beg to differ," she said, slipping her gun free. She clutched it in her palms. "Tell me where my mother is and I'll let you walk out of here. You have my word."

"You have to stop chasing me." His voice sounded as though it were coming from her right.

She pushed to stand, ignoring the lights on the ceiling. "That's not going to happen."

"These are dangerous people. You're going to get hurt."

She punched in some numbers on her biofeed, changing her contacts to see in night vision.

She scanned in the direction of his voice until she found his location. A smile twitched on her lips as she aimed first at his chest and then lowered to point at his leg and pulled the trigger.

Kate Allenton's books are all available in *Kindle Unlimited*.

BETRAYAL (Book 2)
UNTAMED (Book 3)
GUIDED LOYALTY (Book 4)

CARRINGTON-HILL INVESTIGATIONS
DECEPTION (Book 1)
DEADLY DESIRE (Book 2)

SHIFTER PARADISE BOX SET
NOT MY SHIFTER/ SINFULLY CURSED

KARMA

SOPHIE MASTERSON SERIES/ DIXON
SECURITY
LIFTING THE VEIL (Book 1)
BEYOND THE VEIL (Book 2)
VEILED INTENTIONS (Book 3)
VEILED THREATS (Book 4)

THE LOVE FAMILY SERIES
SKYLAR (BOOK1)
DECLAN (BOOK 2)
FLYNN (BOOK 3)
REED (BOOK 4)
LANDON (BOOK 5)
ALEXIS (BOOK 6)
GABE (BOOK 7)
JACKSON (BOOK 8)

LINKED INC.
DEADLY INTENT (BOOK 1)
PSYCHIC LINK (BOOK 2)
PSYCHIC CHARM (BOOK 3)
PSYCHIC GAMES (BOOK 4)
DEADLY DREAMS (BOOK 5)

CREE BLUE PSYCHIC EYE
DEAD WRONG (BOOK 1)
DEADLY VOWS (BOOK 2)
DEAD FAMOUS (BOOK 3)
DEADLY TIES (BOOK 4)
DEADLY BLISS (BOOK 5)
DEADLY FLIRTATION (BOOK 6)

HEX SISTERS
WITCH UNLEASHED (BOOK 1)
WITCHY TROUBLE (BOOK 2)
WITCH BAIT (BOOK 3)

HELL BOUND
MYSTIC TIDES BOX SET
MYSTIC LUCK BOX SET
MAID OF HONOR
HARD SHIFT

ABOUT THE AUTHOR

Kate has lived in Florida for most of her entire life. She enjoys a quiet life with her husband, Michael and two kids.

Kate has pulled all-nighters finishing her favorite books and also writing them. She says she'll sleep when she's dead or when her muse stops singing off key.

She loves creating worlds full of suspense, secrets, hunky men, kick ass heroines, steamy sex and oh yeah the love of a lifetime. Not to mention an occasional ghost and other supernatural talents thrown into the mix.

Sign up for her newsletters at www.kateallenton.com

She loves to hear from her readers by email at KateAllenton@hotmail.com, on Twitter@KateAllenton and on Facebook at facebook.com/kateallenton.1

Visit her website at www.kateallenton.com